"The SQ will show themselves. They always do."

Cave of Wonders

Matthew J. Kirby

SCHOLASTIC INC.

To all those who teach and study history,
I thank you
— M.K.

Copyright © 2013 by Scholastic Inc.

Library of Congress Cataloging-in-Publication Data available

ISBN 978-0-545-48460-2
10 9 8 7 6 5 4 3 2 1   13 14 15 16 17

Cover illustration by Michael Heath
Book design by Keirsten Geise
Back cover photography of characters by Michael Frost © Scholastic Inc.

Library edition, September 2013
Printed in China   62

Scholastic US: 557 Broadway · New York, NY 10012
Scholastic Canada: 604 King Street West · Toronto, ON M5V 1E1
Scholastic New Zealand Limited: Private Bag 94407 · Greenmount, Manukau 2141
Scholastic UK Ltd.: Euston House · 24 Eversholt Street · London NW1 1DB

Have you seen in all the length and breadth of the earth
A city such as Baghdad?
—Umara ibn Aqil, ninth-century poet

Caravans and Camels

THE DESERT wind whipped around them, stirring up sand. Dak shielded his eyes and used his shirt to cover his mouth to keep from breathing in the grit. Sera and Riq did the same. They were standing in the middle of a dusty road, the three of them having just warped from the Great Wall in Ming-dynasty China. For Dak, the prickling, sickening disorientation of having his body squeezed through time and space like a basketball through a keyhole hadn't faded yet . . . and neither had his excitement.

"Where are we?" he asked.

This was their twelfth warp together. You'd think by now, Dak would be used to it, but that question still thrilled him.

Where are we?

What would they see and do? Who would they meet? So far, Christopher Columbus, Vikings, King Louis with his wonderful gooey cheese, Harriet Tubman, the ancient

Maya. People and cultures Dak had only read about in books before now.

Sera checked the Infinity Ring before tucking it away in her satchel. "Coordinates are right. We should be near the city of Baghdad on January 27, the year 1258."

"Good." Dak reached to pull out the SQuare. "Let's figure out the Break we're supposed to fix here."

"Hold on." Riq coughed. "Let's get out of this wind. All this sand won't be good for the SQuare."

"Oh. Right." Dak looked around, and then realized he had just agreed with one of Riq's suggestions without arguing or mocking it. Sera would be so proud. He turned to her. "Bet you're glad I've got the SQuare in my pants, now, huh?"

Sera rolled her eyes at him. "Which way should we go?"

Riq pointed. "I think I see something that way."

The three of them peered down the road, straining to see anything through the windblown sand. Dak was trying to decide how best to make fun of Riq in this moment, when a horrible grunting sounded right behind them.

The three of them spun around to find themselves face-to-face with the protruding nose, huge teeth, and flapping lips of a camel.

The man riding the camel shook his fist at them, shouting in a language Dak didn't recognize. He wore long robes, and a turban coiled around his head.

"Arabic," Riq whispered.

Dak and Sera cocked their heads at the same time as their translation devices kicked in.

The man threw his arms up. "Are you deaf? I said, get out of the road!"

The camel blared at them again. Spit flew out of its open mouth. Its breath smelled bad, and not in the good way a nice cheese smells bad. In the *bad* bad way. Sera plugged her nose while Riq pulled her and Dak off to the side. The rider passed them, and behind him came others. Many others. Most of the camels bore huge bundles slung over their humps.

It was a caravan. An actual camel caravan! At the sight of them, facts bubbled up in Dak's mind. That's how it felt. Like bubbles in a soda, or a burp. They just rose up, and he couldn't keep them in, even though he knew it annoyed most people. "Those bundles are probably filled with spices and silks and frankincense and stuff like that. Baghdad was on the Silk Road trade route, and—"

"Dak!" Sera and Riq both said.

He winced inside. Same as always.

"Sorry." He shrugged. "At least we know which way the city is. I bet this caravan is going there now."

Sera and Riq nodded their agreement with him. So they set off down the road with the caravan, walking through the sandy wind alongside the smelly camels.

Neither Sera nor Riq said much along the way. Dak was used to Riq not talking much with him. They'd become better friends than they were in the beginning, after fixing the first few Breaks together. But the dude still got on Dak's nerves. A lot. So he didn't mind that he was being so quiet right now.

But Sera.

Sera's silence worried him. Normally, he could practically read her thoughts, like she could his. But lately, she felt very far away, and he had no idea what was going on inside her head. There was something she wasn't telling him. He knew it. But he didn't know what that was, and that really bothered him.

The other travelers on the road didn't seem to take any particular notice of them. Dak figured that was because they were still wearing their clothes from China, which was also on the Silk Road, and people here probably saw clothing from China all the time. For once, Dak, Sera, and Riq didn't look so out of place. Or out of time. Dak was glad, too, that their Chinese clothes were relatively thick and warm. It was wintertime here, and the desert air was surprisingly cool.

Baghdad turned out to be less than a mile away. It soon loomed up out of the dust and sand. The wind died down as they passed through the city outskirts, where some buildings were constructed in stone, but most were made out of mud bricks. They crossed several canals, and passed houses with thick walls, low doors, and narrow windows, a design perfect for life in this climate. They crossed open squares where people gathered around wells and in the shade of palm trees.

Ahead of them, the outer walls of the city rose up, high and imposing, reminding Dak of a really huge sand castle.

More facts bubbled in Dak's head. "Baghdad was built not far from where Babylon used to be, and it was one of the greatest centers of learning in all the world, with giant libraries holding thousands of books. This was a Golden Age for the Middle East, while Europe was in the Dark Ages."

Riq turned to look at him. Dak kept going before he could interrupt.

"Scholars and philosophers from all over the world traveled here just so they could study, and everyone worked side by side, no matter where they came from, or what religion they belonged to. The most important thing to them was knowledge."

Riq was still staring at him. Dak waited for him to make fun of him, getting ready to fire something back. But Riq didn't say anything. He just . . . stared.

"What?" Dak asked.

Riq shook his head. "I just don't get why you like history so much."

That caught Dak by surprise. How could someone *not* like history? It was everyone else who was weird, including Riq, and even Sera. But then again, Dak didn't understand why Riq loved languages so much, or why Sera was so into science and math. So, why *did* Dak like history so much? He realized he couldn't exactly answer the question Riq had just raised.

They soon arrived at a city gate where many caravans and travelers merged, jostling Dak from all sides. He heard the others around them call it the Khurâsân Gate. It was only after joining the crowd that Dak noticed the guards standing watch with their metal helmets and swords. They were collecting a toll from everyone who entered the city.

"Um, guys?" Dak stopped in the road.

"What are we going to do?" Sera asked. She had obviously seen them, too. "We don't have any money."

But before they could come up with an answer, the pressing crowd behind them drove them forward. Dak looked around, frantic, but there was no way to escape. The traffic going into the city had caught them in its current, and with each moment brought them closer to the guards.

"Just act natural," Riq whispered. "We've faked our way out of worse stuff than this."

He was right about that. Dak took a deep breath.

They shuffled forward behind the large caravan they'd met on the road, and before long, they were almost to the guards' station. The leader of the caravan, the man who had yelled at them earlier, got off his camel and went to the guards to pay the group's toll.

"I have an idea." Riq moved forward. "Follow my lead. Stay close together."

Dak and Sera glanced at each other, and went with Riq. He led them in between the camels, mixing in with the other members of the caravan. It was a good plan, to try to blend in, but Dak found himself forced right up against the backside of a camel, its tail whipping him in the face, and it smelled even worse than the other camel's front had.

"We better not be here for too long!" he hissed.

Sera and Riq both suppressed smiles.

One of the caravan riders noticed them and looked down, scowling.

Riq gave him a sheepish shrug. "Sorry. Busy day at the Khurâsân Gate."

The rider snorted.

After that, the three of them kept their heads down and remained quiet. And when the caravan started moving, they moved with it, staying as hidden as they could. Dak risked a glance at the guards when they reached them, but the men seemed to already be looking beyond the caravan on to the next travelers.

"It worked!" Dak whispered.

"Of course it worked," Riq said, and then Dak regretted saying anything.

They passed under the shadow of the gate's high arches, through the city wall, and into a busy street where a cacophony of sights and smells and sounds assaulted them. Buildings rose up several stories to either side, sprouting tents and canopies at their bases. Shopkeepers and street vendors shouted their wares.

"The sweetest dates you'll ever taste!"

"Olives! Plump, rich olives!"

"Come! Run your hands over the finest silk between Samarkand and Damascus!"

"The brightest lapis and jasper your eyes have ever seen!"

The sharp smell of spices filled Dak's nose, mixed with that of smoke and camel and other things he couldn't place. It was overwhelming, and amazing. He felt like Aladdin, and could almost believe there was a lamp somewhere waiting for them with a genie in it.

"Wow," Sera said. "Okay. Let's find a quiet place to pull out the SQuare."

"You!"

The three of them turned to see one of the guards marching toward them.

He pointed at them. "You three! Stop!"

"Uh-oh," Dak said.

2

The Riddle of the Cave

THE GUARD had one hand on the pommel of the sword he wore at his waist. "Did you pay the toll?"

"We were with the caravan that just passed through." Riq tried to sound confident. His skill with languages meant he usually ended up being the spokesman. *And let's face it,* he thought, looking at the other two, *that's probably a good thing.* "The leader of our caravan paid the toll."

The guard looked all three of them over, and took his time doing it. "They came from Medina. How is it you are wearing the clothing of China?"

"We spent time there before joining up with that caravan," Riq said.

The guard didn't seem to be buying it. He kept looking at their clothes. "You're pretty young to be working caravans."

For a moment, Riq worried that maybe the man was a Time Warden, an undercover SQ agent on the lookout for time travelers, and his heart began to pound. But he tried to hide it, and told himself to stop being paranoid. "We . . . uh, travel with our parents."

The guard narrowed his eyes.

"Yeah," Dak said. "They're silk traders."

"And they'll be expecting us," Sera said.

The guard released the pommel of his sword. "All right. Get moving, then."

The three of them nodded and turned away. They walked down the street together, and Riq could feel the guard staring at them, his gaze a weight on the back of his neck.

"He's watching us, isn't he?" Sera asked.

Riq peered over his shoulder. "Yup. Just keep moving."

"Do you think he was a Time Warden?" Dak asked.

Riq shook his head. "We can't assume that everyone who looks at us funny is a Time Warden. We tend to get a lot of funny looks."

Dak looked down at his Chinese clothing. "I guess maybe we need to find some clothes that will help us blend in better. The good news is that Baghdad at this time was a diverse place. I mean, it was on the Silk Road, after all."

"The Silk Road?" Sera echoed.

"Duh, like I said before. The Silk Road was a trading route stretching from the Mediterranean all the way to China. Meaning Baghdad had people from all over the world coming through here. We don't have to pretend to be locals, we just might want to look a little less . . . exotic."

Sera glanced around. "I think we need to check out the SQuare before we do anything about clothes. We need to figure out the Break."

"Oh, yeah." Dak pointed at an alleyway nearby. "How about over there?"

Riq nodded. "Looks good."

The three of them crossed the busy street and entered the alley. It was narrow, filled with deep shadows, and aside from a few baskets, it was empty. Dak pulled the SQuare out of his pants, and Riq expected Sera to say something about how gross that was. But she just took the device from Dak with a blank expression. Riq wondered what was going on with her. She wasn't acting like herself. Maybe something was happening with her Remnants, those strange feelings and false memories that came in waves and hinted that something . . . wasn't how it was supposed to be.

"Okay." She flipped on the SQuare and peered at the screen.

Riq waited for her to tell them what she saw there. It was usually some kind of Art of Memory puzzle or a coded message protecting what little information the Hystorians had managed to load onto the device.

"Listen to this." She read it out loud:

"To find what Aristotle gave
Speak the words, open the cave.

Inside a treasure gleaming bright,
The jewels of learning, history's light."

The SQuare let out a little bleep, and an empty box popped up.

"Weird." Sera's eyebrows knitted together. "It looks like it wants a password for something."

"For what?" Dak asked.

Riq peered over Sera's shoulder. "Try *password*. That's what worked before."

"Wait, wait." Dak held his hand out over the screen. "Is this one threatening to blow up if we don't get it right?"

"No." Sera typed. "Okay, *password* didn't work. Any other ideas?"

Riq had no ideas. But the riddle had mentioned something about history. Which meant it was kind of Dak's thing. The kid was annoying, but every once in a while one of those endless, useless facts he pulled out actually helped. "See what Dak can do with it."

Dak nodded. "Let me see it."

Sera handed him the SQuare. He read over the riddle again, and within moments Riq could see him getting all excited. When he got talking about history, he kind of rocked back and forth on his heels.

"Okay. Aristotle," Dak said. "He was the one who founded the Hystorians back in 336 BC. His writings helped uncover the existence of the Great Breaks in history. That *could* be what the riddle means about what Aristotle 'gave.' Or, it could also be referring to how

Aristotle's writings influenced the great minds of Europe during the Renaissance."

Riq sighed. Sifting through all the facts for the useful one sometimes took a while. "That's great, Dak. What else you got?"

"Well, it says 'Speak the words, open the cave.' We *are* in Baghdad. That line of the riddle might refer to the tale of Ali Baba, which, by the way, some believe was *not* one of the original tales from the *One Thousand and One Nights*. Same with *Aladdin*, which was originally set in China. But it would make sense with the 'treasure gleaming bright.' I'm not sure what that would make the 'jewels of learning,' though." He tapped his chin. "I'm going to try something."

"What?" Riq asked.

"Open sesame."

Sera raised an eyebrow. "Actually, that sounds right, with the cave and all."

Dak nodded and typed it in. The SQuare's screen flashed. And then something else came up. "Guys?" Dak held the device out. "Check this out."

Arin Cole appeared on the screen. She was one of Riq's fellow Hystorians, the one who had tried to load all the information they would need about the Great Breaks onto the SQuare. It appeared to be a prerecorded video, created before the attack on the Hystorians' headquarters. She looked stressed, as usual. *More* stressed than usual, in fact.

"He-hello," she said. "Dak and Sera and the rest of our insertion team."

The sight of her, thoughts of the old HQ, it all made Riq think about how he'd grown as a Hystorian. About what he'd given up for the mission.

Kisa. His first true friend, the girl he'd left behind during their mission in the time of the Maya. The girl who had become the first Hystorian to her people. Riq missed her. When he thought of her, he felt the pain and longing of a different kind of Remnant, and he had to take a deep breath to drive it out and focus on the recording.

"If you are watching this," Arin said, "you have reached the Great Break in Baghdad, in the year 1258."

Riq, Sera, and Dak all looked at one another. That was true. They were in the right place. So far, so good.

"That's the good news." Arin sighed. "Now the bad news. In two days, Mongols under the leadership of Hulagu Khan, the grandson of Ghengis Khan, will sack Baghdad. The city will be decimated."

Okay, that *was* bad news. Riq thought back to Paris when the Vikings had laid siege to it, and did not like the thought of going through that kind of thing again.

"During the destruction of the city, hundreds of thousands of books will be destroyed, including those in the House of Wisdom."

"What's the House of Wisdom?" Riq asked.

Dak perked up. "Oh! The House of Wis—"

"*Shh!*" Sera looked hard at both of them. "Do you mind?"

"The House of Wisdom contained a library," Arin said, "with many of the writings of our founder, Aristotle. The Mongols emptied the library and threw all the books in the Tigris River. Among the books they destroyed was a volume of Aristotle's research on the Great Breaks. Specifically, research pertaining to the very first Great Break—or, from your perspective, the *last* Great Break. The final one you will fix."

Riq leaned closer. If the Hystorians didn't have the volume about the last Great Break . . .

Sera shook her head. "But if the book was lost—?"

"Shh!" Riq said.

"Without that book," Arin said, "that first, crucial Great Break—the Prime Break—will be impossible to fix, and our entire mission will be lost. New Breaks will occur faster than you can fix them. The Earth will be destroyed in the Cataclysm. We Hystorians knew this day would come, when our knowledge of the Prime Break would have to be saved."

"Great," Dak said. "No pressure or anything."

"Shh!" Riq and Sera said at the same time.

"Your task," Arin said, "is to save the library at the House of Wisdom, and with it the writings of Aristotle. It is the only way to save the world."

Arin stepped aside, and then Brint and Mari walked into view on the recording. Riq hadn't seen them since the SQ had attacked them all, before their first Break saving Christopher Columbus from a mutiny.

"We want to express our gratitude and admiration,"

Brint said. "If you've made it this far, you've fixed eight of the Breaks. Only a handful more to go before the Prime Break."

Eight done. Only a few left. As Riq thought about that, a dread seeped into him about what would happen to him when they finished. He knew he had messed with his family tree back in 1850. He didn't even know if he technically existed anymore. . . .

It didn't help that the people in the video, people he'd known all his life, weren't addressing him by name. But he told himself that was just because he had joined Dak and Sera's mission at the very last second.

Mari spoke next. "After you have fixed the Baghdad Break, and saved the information we need on the Prime Break, you will face the most dangerous part of your mission so far."

More dangerous than a Mongol invasion? Riq froze, waiting for what Mari would say next. So, it seemed, did Sera and Dak.

"Your current SQuare has no information on the Prime Break," Mari said, "because we didn't have any information to load on it. If you fix the Baghdad Break in the past, we will have that information in the present. That means you will have to return to the present for a new SQuare at some point."

Riq's whole body felt like he'd just walked outside into the snow in his pajamas. Every Hystorian knew that once you entered the time stream, it would be extremely dangerous to warp back to the present before all the Breaks were fixed. There was no telling what would happen. Paradoxes. Holes ripped in the fabric of reality. The end of the universe. But Riq had something else to be afraid of.

"We know it's a risk," Mari said.

You have no idea. If Riq went back to the future *now,* he might cease to exist.

"But it's one we have to take," Brint said. "There is no other choice. Hopefully, by this point, history will be repaired enough to cope with the potential paradoxes."

Riq swallowed. *What if it isn't?*

"Good luck," Mari said. "And one last thing. Arin?"

"There's *more*?" Dak threw up his hands. "Isn't that enough?!"

Mari and Brint stepped aside, and Arin came back on the screen, clutching an armful of papers.

"Yes." She adjusted her glasses. "I'm sorry. I've done countless hours of research. Really, you have no idea. I mean, if you could see the mountain of parchment I—"

"Arin." That was Mari's voice off to the side. "It might help if you could get to the point."

"Right." Arin cleared her throat. "Unfortunately, we have no idea who the Hystorian in Baghdad was. You're on your own."

The Streets of Baghdad

THE SCREEN went black. Sera stared at it. Really the message from Arin could not have been any worse. Of all of them, Sera was the only one who had *seen* the Cataclysm. She'd witnessed firsthand what would happen to the world if they failed in their mission to repair the Breaks. She also knew that somehow, she had parents now, in the future, a mother and father who had only been Remnants before Sera, Dak, and Riq had begun their mission. Before they'd changed the past. Parents who would die in the flooding, ripped away from Sera just as she'd become aware of them.

But if she had to go back to the future for a new SQuare, would they be there? Would she be able to meet them?

"So, let's get to it," Dak said. "We have a Hystorian to find. I bet he'll be at the House of Wisdom with Aristotle's books, don't you think?"

How could Dak just move on like that? Didn't he realize

what was happening? Sera's irritation got the better of her. "How do you know it's a *he* and not a *she*, Dak? Huh? Why do you assume that?"

Dak shrugged, his eyes downward. "I don't know. Geez, what's the matter with you? What's the matter with both of you?"

"Nothing," Sera and Riq said at the same time.

Sera looked at Riq. He was frowning, his forehead creased in worry. When he looked back at her, Sera saw that Arin's message had obviously disturbed him, too. Maybe it had something to do with his Remnants. She knew he had them like she did. They'd talked about them before.

"Fine," Dak said. "Don't tell me."

"Oh, for the love of mincemeat," Sera said. "Quit pouting, all right?" Maybe it would be best to just get moving and not think about all that other stuff. Put the Cataclysm out of her mind and concentrate on the mission. The Break. The really, really important Break on which everything depended. Sera sighed. "The House of Wisdom seems like a good place to start. Don't you think so, Riq?"

"Yeah." Riq's voice was quiet. "Sounds good."

"Well—" Dak looked back and forth between them. "Okay, then."

Sera took the SQuare and tucked it away. They left the alley, returning to the main street with its seemingly endless stream of pedestrians and camels. She had to admit, it was pretty exciting to be here, and not too different from what she'd imagined it would be like. Except for the noise, which was louder than she would have expected.

"Okay," Riq said. "Directions." He stopped someone walking past and asked him about the House of Wisdom. The man gestured and pointed, his hand going one way, then the other. Sera couldn't really hear him, so she hoped Riq got it all.

Riq thanked the man, and then said, "Let's go. It's on the other side of the city. We'll try to find some clothes on the way."

Clothes. Sera looked around, trying to figure out what girls and women wore here, but quickly saw there were a lot more men on the street than women. The men all seemed to be wearing about the same thing. Layers of fabric of different patterns and colors, robes with wide sleeves and wide belts, and most of them wore some kind of wrapping or turban around their head. Things would be easy for Dak and Riq. But it looked like it would be harder for Sera. The women wore a wider variety of styles. Some wore plain dresses, or dresses that were brocaded or embroidered, and some wore flowing silks in vivid colors. Some dressed in black with veils that covered their hair and their faces. Still others wore scarves and beaded headdresses.

"What am I supposed to wear?" she asked out loud.

"Take your pick," Dak said. "You should be happy. Lots of cultures and religions mean lots of choices for once!"

"Come on," Riq said. He set off down the busy road.

Dak shrugged at Sera, and they followed after him.

The road ran a straight course ahead of them, but off to either side, it seemed to Sera the city stretched away in a maze of narrow, twisting streets. The buildings climbed up high, some with balconies surrounded with wooden screens, and canopies that reached out above them.

"It's so loud." Sera almost felt like she had to shout over the camels, the donkeys, and the shop owners.

"I know, isn't it great?!" Dak grinned.

They soon came to an enormous archway spanning the road. It almost looked like an older version of the city gate they had just come through, except it was standing by itself in the street, without any walls connected to it. They walked under it, and entered an open square in front of a building that was much larger than the rest. It stood apart, decorated with paint and iridescent tiles.

Sera turned to Dak. "What do you think that is?"

"I don't know," he said.

"It's a college," Riq said, scowling.

"Good call! Baghdad had — has — a lot of colleges," Dak said. "And a lot of libraries. In fact, there was this one rich guy whose *personal* library took four hundred camels to move. Even I think that's a lot of books for one dude."

"But we need to find a specific library," Sera said. "And a specific book."

Riq shook his head. "Let's keep moving."

Sera grunted. She didn't know what was going on with Riq, and she was trying to be patient, but she was kind of getting annoyed.

Not much farther, the road turned sharply to the left, a canal running alongside it, sometimes visible, sometimes underground. Sera couldn't even see the end of the street off in the distance. This city was huge. They walked ahead for what would have been three or four blocks back home, and before long, all the sights and smells and sounds started to overwhelm her. How were they going to find a single Hystorian in all of this?

"I think I see another one of those gates." Dak pointed down the street.

Sera squinted. "I think you're right."

"They must be pretty old," Dak said. "From when the city was smaller, with a whole different wall around it or something. And now all that's left are these gates."

As they got closer to this one, a metallic clanging pierced the air. It sounded like a large group of people was banging a whole bunch of pots and pans together. The three of them looked at one another.

Then Riq leaned toward a passerby. "Excuse me, but what is that up ahead?"

The man looked back over his shoulder. "The Archway of the Armorers, of course."

Armor. If blacksmiths were making armor up there, that explained the sound. It also made Sera wish she had some earplugs, because the noise only got louder the closer they got.

This archway was in better condition than the last one had been. Decorations covered much of it, swirling patterns pressed into the clay bricks, with more of the iridescent tiles. Up close, they swirled with golds, greens, and browns. The archway still had its gate, too, but it was open, and they walked through it.

"Cool!" Dak said. "Look at that!"

Blacksmiths stood at forges and workbenches near one side of the square, shaping sheets of metal into what looked to Sera like helmets, and bending metal wire into rings, which they linked together into shirts of chain mail.

The people around here mostly seemed like soldiers, or guards, and as Sera passed by them, she overheard snippets of conversation.

"Hulagu and his Mongol horde are only a few days from the city."

"What about the caliph's cavalry?"

"Defeated. Wiped out."

"All of them?"

"All twenty thousand."

Sera's eyes widened. She knew a little bit about the Mongols. She knew they rode horses, and that the Great

Wall of China, where the three of them had just been fixing another Great Break, was built to keep the Mongols out. But to think of them wiping out twenty thousand soldiers, and now approaching the city, dropped a chunk of ice in her stomach.

"Did you hear that?" she asked Dak and Riq. "We don't have much time."

"I've been looking for an opportunity to score some clothes," Riq said. "I haven't seen anything."

"I might have an idea," Dak said. "But I need a quiet spot."

Quiet? What was Dak thinking of doing? Sera never knew with him, and usually, that was exciting and fun. It was part of why they were friends. She liked seeing what crazy ideas he came up with, but that was back home. Here in Baghdad, when the fate of the world was at stake, they didn't need one of Dak's turned-out-to-not-be-such-a-good-idea ideas.

The crowded road past the Archway of the Armorers continued as far as the eye could see. They pressed their way down it, the equivalent of another three or four blocks, until they came to the biggest gate they had seen so far. It was a couple of stories tall, covered in more of the decorations and shimmering tiles. It arched over the opening to a large square, while the road continued on to the left.

"We go through the arch," Riq said. "According to that guy's directions."

So they passed under its shadow, and the square opened up a wide patch of blue sky above. Sera felt like she could breathe again. She inhaled, and smelled new fragrances on the breeze: herbs, flowers, and perfumes. At the far side of the square stood a beautiful mosque. Sera recognized it as a mosque because of the minaret, the tall tower beside it.

"That's the mosque of the caliph," Riq said.

"Who's the caliph?" Sera asked.

"He was a religious leader of Islam," Dak said.

The mosque had a high wall around it, decorated in bright blue hues that glinted like a lake in the sun. Onion-shaped domes crowned the wall's four corners.

"He was also the ruler of Baghdad." Dak pointed across the square. "And I bet that's his palace."

Beyond the mosque, another city wall surrounded the edge of the square, and beyond that, Sera saw an even larger building. It was decorated with reds, blues, and purples, its many domes and towers forming an imposing skyline over the city.

"That wall surrounds a couple of palaces like that one," Riq said. "And a college, and the House of Wisdom."

"So, how do we get inside?" Dak asked.

"The Gate of the Willow Tree," Riq said. "The directions said it's that way." He pointed down a street in the far corner of the square.

They set off toward it. Sera was grateful for the open space, and the ability to walk without having to dodge oncoming camels. It was a bit warmer out in the sun, and the pleasant smell she'd noticed earlier just got stronger. When they reached the street Riq had pointed at, she realized why.

It was a whole market of perfume makers. The fragrances of basil and other herbs hung in the air, the scent of spices and oils and aromas Sera couldn't identify. Sweet smells, sharp smells, and pungent, musky smells. There were more women here, too, outside the perfume shops.

"We just go through here," Riq said, "and then . . . Where's Dak?"

Sera spun around. He had just been right there beside her, and now he was gone. She scanned the market and spotted him over by a lemon and orange vendor.

"There he is," she said. "What's he doing?"

Dak climbed up onto a tall basket and held out his hands. "Come!" he shouted. "Listen to me!"

"Oh, no," Sera whispered. This must have been his idea, the one he needed quiet for, and she could already tell it was going to be a bad one.

4

The Market Inspector

DAK NOTICED immediately that Sera and Riq were staring at him. Sera, especially, looked worried. Maybe he should have told them what he was about to do before he did it. But they never seemed to like Dak's ideas, even though sometimes, his ideas worked out really, really well. Other times . . .

"Come, come!" As he shouted from his basket, a curious crowd gathered around him.

Dak knew they needed clothes, and to get some, they needed money, because so far, he hadn't seen any clothes just lying around waiting for them to come along. He'd been going over what he knew about Baghdad, trying to figure out what they could do to earn some cash, when an idea came to him.

He remembered that there were storytellers who performed on the streets. They hadn't seen one yet, but Dak didn't see why *he* couldn't try to tell a story. If people liked it and they tossed him a few coins, maybe they'd be able to buy some clothes.

But now that he was up there, with a bunch of people looking at him, waiting, he wondered if he'd made a mistake.

"Uh . . . Now I will tell you a story!" He waved his hand in an arc in front of him. He didn't know why. It just seemed like a storyteller thing to do. "Once . . . upon a time!"

Sera slapped her forehead. Riq folded his arms across his chest.

"There was a djinn." Dak congratulated himself for using the real word for genie. "And this djinn . . ." What? What should his story be about? Dak realized he probably should have figured that out before he got up here, but it was too late to back down now. So he grabbed the first thing that came into his mind. "This djinn had a ring that had magical powers. It allowed the djinn to travel backward in time!"

Sera was shaking her head now. Riq's mouth hung open. What was their problem?

"One day," Dak said, "the djinn met . . . a man. In the desert. And the man was wandering around, lost and depressed. And the djinn goes, 'Why are you wandering around lost and depressed?' And the man, uh, the man goes, 'Oh, I'm sad because my house burned down, and the fire destroyed . . . a book my parents gave to me. It was my prized possession.'"

Dak thought he was doing a pretty good job. The audience seemed to be interested. None of them had walked away yet. So he kept going.

"When the djinn heard this, he said, 'I can grant you your heart's desire. What is it?' And the man was like, 'Really? My heart's desire is to have my book back.' So the djinn used his magical ring and took them both back in time to the man's house *before* the fire."

Hey, this story is actually pretty good! But Dak noticed a man standing at the back of the audience who did not look so happy. He wore a gray robe over a striped one, with a bright red turban wrapped around his head. Two fairly big guys — city guards by the look of them — stood on either side of him, and all three of them were glaring at Dak.

He kept going. "And they snuck into the man's house, and the man from the future wanted to warn the man from the past about the fire, but the djinn was all, 'No. You said your heart's desire was your book.'" Dak felt his voice getting louder, and the words came faster. "So they went to the man's library, and they found the book his parents had given to him, and they took it, and the djinn used his ring to take them both back to the future where they came from. And the man had saved the book, his one true desire. The end."

Dak bowed low.

No one clapped. He looked up. A moment later, he heard the light clink of a metal coin hitting the ground in front of him. Then another and another. The audience broke up, going back to whatever it was they'd stopped doing to listen to him.

Dak hopped down from his basket, feeling proud, and collected the money he'd earned. He didn't recognize the coins, and he didn't know how much was there, but he didn't care right then. As he picked up the last, Sera and Riq rushed up to him.

"What were you thinking?" Sera was talking in that hissing voice she used when she was mad at him but couldn't yell because there were teachers around.

"What do you mean?" He held out his handful of coins. "Look!"

"That's great," Riq said. "But what about that thing you just did where you told the whole city about the Infinity Ring, and why we're here?"

"I didn't do that," Dak said.

Sera lifted an eyebrow at him. "Magical ring that goes backward in time? Saving a book from a fire?"

Dak looked at the coins in his hand. "I *did* do that, didn't I?" How could he have not realized he was basically turning their mission into a story? "Oops. What do we do now?"

"Hope there wasn't a Time Warden in the audience," Sera said.

"Uh-oh." Dak remembered that guy with the red turban, and started looking around for him.

"'Uh-oh' what?" Riq asked.

Dak spotted him. He and his two guards were stalking toward them, and they looked even less happy than they had before. "'Uh-oh' him."

"You! Storyteller!" The man in the red turban pointed at Dak. "Hold it right there."

"What seems to be the trouble?" Riq asked.

"The trouble," the man said, "is that I don't remember issuing a permit for this young man to tell stories on the street." He had a long, pointed beard and very deep-set eyes.

"You need a permit to tell a story?" Dak asked. "Really?"

"I am the Market Inspector!" The man's glare trampled over all three of them. "And I decide what you need a permit for, and, yes, you need a permit to be a public entertainer. Do you have a permit?"

Dak gave a little shrug. "Well, no."

The Market Inspector put his hands on his hips. "Then you must forfeit your illicit gain. Turn over the money."

Dak didn't want to. He had earned it. He had found a way to maybe buy some clothes. "Look, I'm sorry, I didn't know. Can't you just let it go this one time?"

The man's eyes got sharp and narrow. "I *never* let things go."

Dak looked at Sera and Riq. They looked back at him. He flicked his eyes in the direction Riq had pointed before. They nodded.

"Well, sir, I'm sorry," Dak said. "If I'd known I needed a permit, I would have — RUN!" Dak launched into a sprint across the square, Sera and Riq close behind him.

"Seize them!" the Market Inspector shouted.

Dak looked back and saw the two city guards barreling after them as they left the Perfume Market and dove into the city.

The streets got narrower. They twisted and turned like a maze, climbing up and down steps, and they were as crowded as ever with camels and donkeys. People shouted at the three time travelers as they ran past, bumping into things. Dak accidentally knocked over a cart full of bread.

"Sorry!" he shouted over his shoulder.

Riq ran up alongside Dak. "Let me lead the way!"

He turned them down one street, then another. Dak soon lost all sense of direction, and he hoped Riq knew where he was going. But no matter how many turns they made or how far they ran, they just couldn't seem to dodge the Market Inspector and the guards, who stayed right behind them.

"Apparently," Sera shouted, "he really *doesn't* let anything go!"

"Keep running!" Riq shouted.

Eventually, they burst onto a busier, wider street. There were even more people and animals here. More stalls and carts and shops. There was an old guy sitting on the ground nearby selling rugs, which he had laid out in stacks in front of his shop.

"I have an idea!" Sera looked back, and then led them to the rugs. She dropped to the ground, grabbed the edge of one of the rugs, and rolled herself up in it. Dak grinned and did the same thing.

"You have got to be kidding me," Riq said, but soon he was rolled up in a rug, too.

The three of them lay there, side by side like burritos, while the rug seller just stared in surprise. Dak wiggled a hand free and flicked him one of the coins he'd just earned, then put his finger in front of his lips to say, "Shh."

The old guy caught the coin, looked at it, and then glanced up as the Market Inspector charged out into the street. The rug seller winked at Dak, and looked away. Dak smiled, then ducked back inside his rug and tried to hold completely still.

Several moments passed. The sounds of the street carried on around them. Dak realized he was holding his breath, and at the same time realized he couldn't hold it forever. How long would they have to lie there?

"You, Rug Merchant!" That was the Market Inspector's voice. "We are looking for two children, one a Frank and the other a Persian like you, and an older youth with them, an African. Have you seen them?"

"Yes, *muhtasib,* I have seen them," the rug seller said. Dak went cold inside.

"Well? Where are they?" the Market Inspector asked.

"They ran that way," the rug seller said. "Toward the Gate of the Sultan."

Dak closed his eyes in relief. Then he heard the sound

of several feet beating the road away from them, eventually growing distant and quiet until he couldn't hear them anymore.

"You can come out now, little *pirashki*."

Dak jerked sideways as the old guy lifted the edge of the rug and rolled him out into the street. He got up and dusted himself off as the rug seller did the same with Sera and Riq.

"Now that's what I call a magic carpet," he said.

Riq turned to the merchant. "Thanks for not telling him where we were," he said.

"Bah." The rug seller gave Dak back his coin. "The Market Inspector is a powerful and unpopular man. It pleases me to find ways to frustrate him."

"Thank you," Dak said. "What's your name?"

"Farid," he said. "And you are?"

"I'm Dak. This is Sera and Riq."

"I am happy to meet you," he said. "And now, I do not want to seem rude, but the Market Inspector will realize you have slipped out of his grasp and return this way soon."

"Thanks," Riq said. "We'll get going. Could you tell us the way to the House of Wisdom?"

"Oh, the House of Wisdom is it?" Farid chuckled. "Are you scholars in addition to being rug testers?"

"Yes," Sera said. "I guess we kind of are."

Farid gave them directions, and they said good-bye to him. They weren't as far off track as Dak had worried they would be after their escape from the Market Inspector. Before long, they were standing before the Gate of the Willow Tree, the great palace they had seen before much closer now. They had circled around it.

Riq pointed through the gate. "The House of Wisdom is on the other side."

They'd made it.

The House of Wisdom

RIQ STILL couldn't believe how careless Dak had been. What if there had been a Time Warden in the audience? That could have been the end of the entire mission. As it was, Riq was still worried about the Market Inspector. He had seemed a little too determined to catch them.

Through the gate, they were able to see more of the palace. It was incredible, like something out of those old postcards Riq's Grandma Phoebe had kept from all her travels. Now that they were on this side of the wall, Riq could see there were actually several grand palaces and buildings. Gardens grew between them, lush with different trees and palms, and all kinds of colored flowers, bushes, and plants, while fountains spouted and bubbled in their midst.

Riq pointed to the right. "The first guy I talked to said the House of Wisdom is one of those buildings overlooking the river."

"There's a river running through the city?" Sera asked.

"That would be the Tigris River," Dak said. "Along with the Euphrates River, it forms a part of what's known as the Fertile Crescent region."

Riq rolled his eyes, but he was too tired to even make fun of Dak's history vomit right now.

So Dak kept going. "The region was also known as the 'cradle of civilization,' because it's where some of the first civilizations in the world started. Like the ancient Sumerians. Did you know they had the first system of writing in the world? It's called cuneiform."

"That's great, Dak," Sera said.

"It is, isn't it?" From the sound of it, Dak hadn't picked up on Sera's sarcasm.

"We're almost there. Let's just go. We can worry about new clothes later." Riq hadn't said anything to the other two, but he almost didn't want to get to this House of Wisdom place. Every step he took toward it felt like a step toward a future where he didn't exist anymore. The only thing keeping him moving was his dedication to the mission. It was his way of honoring the memory of Kisa.

They passed in front of a two-story building with a series of striped, pointed arches in the walls. Riq remembered that was another college from the first guy's directions. Beyond the college, they could finally see the Tigris River flowing. It was as wide as maybe four soccer fields. Sailboats and rowboats moved across its surface like bugs. Bustling wharves and piers covered the shoreline, and across the water, Riq could see the western half of Baghdad. The river flowed right through the city, on its way to wherever it went, and it made Riq think about their mission. Fixing the Great Breaks, like removing boulders from the river of time.

"It's big," Sera said.

"This is called the Wharf of the Needle-Makers," Riq said. "And the next building should be the one we're looking for."

Up ahead, past a small courtyard, they saw a large, plain building. Its walls looked sturdy and well kept, but lacked the opulent decorations of the palaces and colleges. It had no windows, and a single large door standing open. Several men milled about in front of the entrance, most of them wearing white turbans.

To the side of the door, Riq saw a single engraving. It read:

بيت الحكمة

"The House of Wisdom," he said, pleased that he'd taken the time to learn how to read and write Arabic. "This is definitely it."

"Okay," Sera said. "So how do we do this?"

"What do you mean?" Dak asked. "We just walk in."

"Oh, for the love of mincemeat," Sera said. "First you go and blab our mission in front of the whole Perfume

Market, and now you're going to just walk in and . . . what? Ask which one of them is a Hystorian? Do you realize there could just as easily be SQ Time Wardens in there?"

"I hadn't thought of that," Dak said.

"I know," Sera said.

"But I would have figured it out," Dak said.

"But not before it was too late," Sera said.

Riq raised his voice to interrupt them. "If we can get in there, the Hystorian may come to us. They're on the lookout for us, remember?"

"But so are Time Wardens," Sera said.

But that didn't make sense to Riq when he thought about it. "Maybe not. Look, the Time Wardens know Aristotle founded the Hystorians, right? I'm betting if there were a Time Warden in the House of Wisdom, they would have destroyed Aristotle's books a long time ago. There wouldn't be anything in there for us to save from the Mongols in the first place."

Dak turned to Sera. "I guess *you* didn't think of *that*!"

"Neither did you!"

"Let's just go in and see what happens," Riq said.

They approached the front door, attracting looks from the men standing around outside it. Riq tried to hold his head up in a way that said the three of them belonged there, and they knew exactly where they were going. But they hadn't reached the door before one of the men called to them.

"Can we help you?" he asked.

"We're here to see the House of Wisdom," Riq said, turning back to face him.

The man nodded up at the building. "Then your purpose has been fulfilled."

Great. This guy was super literal. He was probably a linguist. The annoying kind. "What I meant," Riq said, "is that we have come to visit the scholars within the House of Wisdom."

The man left his group and came over to them. "Is that so?"

Dak piped up. "It is."

"And what is it you seek from us?" the man asked.

"Uh . . ." Dak stuck out his handful of coins. "We've come to make a donation."

The man wrinkled his nose at the money like it smelled funky. "A donation?"

And now Dak had gone and offended him. The kid was on a roll.

"Sure," Dak said. "You guys take donations, right? Don't libraries always need money?"

The man's nostrils flared. "The House of Wisdom does not beg for money."

Now Sera spoke. "But do you take it when someone offers it?"

The man looked back at Dak's hand. "If you wish to contribute to the learning that goes on here, I'm certain such a donation would come back to reward *you* tenfold."

Riq's tension eased. The guy may have been too proud to admit the House of Wisdom needed the money, but he wasn't turning them away.

"For our donation," Riq said, "could we maybe go inside?"

The man looked each of them up and down. "I suppose that would not hurt anything. Follow me."

Riq sighed in relief, and so did Sera.

Dak just grinned. "Open sesame," he whispered.

They followed the man to the door and he ushered them through.

Inside, the building had a huge courtyard in the center, lined with columns and arches, and surrounded by two stories of doors and corridors. Dozens of people moved around, crossing the courtyard, going in and out of doorways, carrying stacks of paper and scrolls and books.

"And now you have been inside," the man said.

"Could we look around a bit?" Dak asked.

The man sucked air through his teeth. "Let me find Abi."

"Who?" Riq asked.

"Ibn Abī al-Shukr. He volunteers to show newcomers around. He enjoys it, for some reason. Wait here."

He walked away, leaving the three of them alone.

"This is amazing," Dak said. "There are probably books in here the people of our time have never seen or even heard of. Think of the history!"

"I'm more interested in the books on math and science," Sera said.

"The only book we're here for is the one that will prevent the Cataclysm," Riq said, even though as he said it, his stomach tightened up.

"Right," Dak said. "But if we happen to *see* another cool book along the way, there's no harm in looking."

Riq shook his head. "Dak, I—"

"Here they are, Abi." The man who had let them in had returned with another man by his side. The new guy was younger, maybe in his late twenties or early thirties. He wore a pale blue robe and a white turban. A thick beard covered his very round face, and his smile seemed wide enough to touch his ears.

"Welcome!" he said.

The other man nodded and left them, back through the front door.

Abi lifted his eyebrows. "I'm told you wish to make a donation and see the House of Wisdom?"

"That's right!" Dak held out his handful of coins.

The man took them with both hands and a slight bow of his head. "I do feel some discomfort taking money from a young man like yourself, but I believe you are sincere, and we thank you for your generosity. I am Ibn Abī al-Shukr, but you may call me Abi."

"I'm Dak. This is Sera and Riq."

"Is that so?" The tone of the man's voice became serious. "Unusual names."

"Yes, well"—Sera put on that innocent smile that Riq had seen her use before—"we're not from here."

"I perceive that," the man said. "I believe you have traveled far. Very far indeed."

Riq thought he seemed suspicious. Was he simply talking about their clothes from China? Or did he mean something else? The first guy had said Abi liked to show newcomers around the place, and now Riq wondered why that was. Could it be because Abi was the Hystorian? Maybe being the designated tour guide let him check to see if any strangers coming to the House of Wisdom were from the future.

Riq decided to test that theory. "We come from farther away than you would probably think. He said you like to show new people around?"

"I do," Abi said. "I . . . have an interest in where people come from, and how and why they find their way here to the House of Wisdom."

"I bet you hear all kinds of stories," Riq said.

"I do." Abi smiled. "But so far, nothing that would seem *impossible* to believe. No one has yet flown here, for example. Or come by other means unknown to the people of my time."

Time. That settled it in Riq's mind. This guy had to be either a Hystorian or a Time Warden, and since he still doubted they'd find any Time Wardens here in the House of Wisdom, the moment had come for them to stick their necks out once again. He looked at Sera and Dak, and gave a little shrug. He was going for it.

"We came here by something you might think is impossible," he said.

"Oh?" Abi asked.

"Yeah, you could say our . . . boat travels *backward* up the river."

Abi cocked his head. "I see. Come, let me show you more of the House of Wisdom."

He gestured for them to follow him, and they proceeded down one of the arched walkways around the courtyard. From there, they took one of the corridors deeper into the building, the scuff of their steps echoing back at them. They passed several spacious rooms, each lined with bookshelves set in arched alcoves with borders of intricate paint and tile around them. Scholars were at work within each of the rooms, reading and writing and speaking in hushed tones.

Riq thought back to the courtyard. If all the corridors were like this, with big rooms full of books, then there were thousands and thousands of volumes here.

Eventually, they came to what Riq assumed was some kind of sitting area. Except there weren't any chairs. Persian rugs covered the floor, and cushions and pillows surrounded a few low tables. It was otherwise empty.

"Please, sit down." Abi gestured toward one of the tables.

Riq, Sera, and Dak all lowered themselves to the floor. It was actually comfortable. Really comfortable. More comfortable than any of the chairs at the Hystorian headquarters, that was for sure. Riq thought he might suggest to Brint and Mari that they start conducting all Hystorian meetings on cushions on the floor. But then he remembered his fears and that thought turned to dread.

"Good. Now we can talk." Abi took a seat across the table from them. "As I'm sure you have guessed, I, like you, am a Hystorian."

Riq didn't know whether that was cause for celebration or despair.

6

Roses

SERA WAS finally able to relax a little. They had found Abi, in spite of Dak, but also because of Dak, and it was quiet here. The walls of the House of Wisdom kept the clamor and chaos of the city out, and Sera thought this was a place she could get some work done. Maybe solve the Riemann hypothesis, which seemed appropriate, since the Babylonians were the first to use the number zero, one of the few history facts that interested Sera.

"So you know why we're here?" Riq asked Abi.

"Of course. You are here from the future to prevent a Great Break from occurring."

"Exactly," Riq said.

Abi leaned forward. "And do you know what this Break is? Does it have to do with Hulagu Khan and the Mongols, who are at our very doorstep?"

"Yes," Dak said. "They're going to sack Baghdad in two days. According to the history books, it's going to be bad. And I mean *really* bad."

"How bad?" Abi asked.

"Baghdad will basically be a ghost town for a few hundred years," Dak said.

Abi sat back, exhaling sharply. "And what of the libraries?"

"The Mongols are going to destroy them," Dak said. "Eyewitnesses said the Tigris River ran black with the ink of all the books they threw in the water."

"No, no, no," Abi whispered, eyes wide, shaking his head. "'The scholar's ink is more sacred than the blood of martyrs.' So said the Prophet, peace be upon him."

It looked to Sera like Abi felt an almost physical pain when he thought about books being destroyed. But Sera had learned among her ancestors just how powerful a single book could be. Books could save cultures, like the Maya. In the case of Aristotle, books could save the world.

"Do you have a plan for how to repair this Break?" Abi asked.

"No," Riq said. "All we know is that we can't let Aristotle's writings be destroyed. Beyond that, we were hoping you might be able to give us some ideas."

Abi took a deep breath. "I think it would be impossible to prevent the Mongols from attacking. They have swept through Persia already, and even conquered the fortress of Alamut, which no force has done in nearly two hundred years."

"What about the caliph?" Riq asked. "Can't he just

talk to Hulagu? Maybe even surrender?"

"Hulagu will attempt to negotiate, but the caliph does not believe the city will fall. He will not see reason. That is why he waited until it was too late before he sent out his cavalry."

Sera remembered what she'd heard at the Archway of the Armorers. "And they were all wiped out." She shuddered. "Okay. So the Mongols are coming and we can't stop them. Can we move the books?"

"No," Abi said. "It would take a thousand camels, and even then, where would we move them to? I've heard the Mongol army is now on both sides of the river." He made a fist. "They have the city in a vise."

"What about just saving Aristotle's book?" Dak asked. "That seems easier, and it's all Brint and Mari needed for the Prime Break, right?"

"How would you save it?" Abi asked.

"I don't know," Dak said. "Just hide it somewhere."

Abi scratched his beard. "And do you think you could find a place where it would be safe for several centuries? How will it be found when it is needed? Who will find it? What if the SQ get to it before then?"

Dak held up his hands. "Okay, okay. I get it."

Sera had another idea. Maybe the safest place for the book was with them. "What if we take it with us?" she asked. "Just take it to Brint and Mari in the present."

"And what happens to my time without it?" Abi asked. "How do you know if by taking it, you are not robbing the intervening centuries of needed knowledge? Books need libraries. Libraries are the vessels of the world's accumulated wisdom."

"So we have to save the library," Riq said. "We may not be able to stop Hulagu from attacking the city. But could we stop him from destroying the libraries?"

"What?" Dak said. "Like, just ask him? 'Hey, Hulagu, what's goin' on, dude? Hey listen, I know you're about to conquer Baghdad and all, but do you think you could leave that library alone? That'd be great. Thanks.'"

"Shut up," Riq said.

"You shut up," Dak said.

"I'm not the one suggesting dumb ideas," Riq said.

"That sure sounded like one to me," Dak said.

Abi looked back and forth between them like someone watching a tennis match played by monkeys.

"Oh, for the love of —" Just when Sera thought these two might be starting to get along, they turned back into bickering second graders, and for the thirty-seventh time she wondered if immaturity was a side effect of time travel. "Both of you, grow up!"

They stopped.

Dak folded his arms, glowering.

Riq clenched his jaw for a few seconds, and then said, "I was just thinking that persuasion might be an option."

"Dumb!" Dak said.

"Actually," Abi said, "you might be close to something."

"You think Hulagu might actually see reason?" Sera asked.

"I have someone else in mind," Abi said. "When

Hulagu conquered the Alamut fortress, he took an imprisoned scholar from there as his advisor. Nasir al-Din al-Tusi."

Sera knew that name. Tusi was a famous astronomer and mathematician, and Sera had studied him. She admired him. The Tusi Couple was really important in Copernicus's model of the solar system and the motions of the planets. And Tusi was with Hulagu Khan?

"The caliph has already refused to surrender," Abi said, "but I have heard that Hulagu will send Tusi to the caliph to attempt to convince him. If we can persuade Tusi, then *he* might have enough influence with Hulagu to get him to spare the library."

"It's worth a shot," Riq said. "Do you know when he'll be here?"

Abi shook his head. "I think very soon. Let me reach out to my contacts in the palace. They will know more."

A short while later, Abi brought them food. Really good food. There were dates, olives, cheese, and flatbread, with a couple of spicy dishes that reminded Sera of curry. They drank water flavored with the juice of melons. While eating around the low tables, they mostly used their fingers and the flatbread to scoop food into their mouths. Dak seemed to really enjoy eating with his hands. And of course, he especially enjoyed the cheese.

"Mm," he said. "It's a goat cheese like feta or chevret, but saltier."

Abi didn't eat, but instead asked them questions about the future world they had come from. Sera was surprised at some of his reactions. He readily accepted some things she thought he might not believe them about, like cars.

"Automata are well known to us," he said. "The Banū Mūsā brothers created many ingenious devices here in the House of Wisdom centuries ago."

But when they talked about the other Great Breaks, Abi grew surprised, and even doubtful. He was especially amazed at their adventure with the Maya.

"Do you mean there is another *land* across the sea that we know nothing about?" he asked.

"Yes." Sera sat up straight when she talked about her ancestors now. "The people there have a powerful empire with an amazing culture."

"And you saved *their* writings, too?" Abi asked.

"Yeah," Riq said. "This is actually the second book we've had to save."

"Not just a book." Abi looked around. "A library."

Dak cleared his throat. "And now you guys see why history is important, right? Not just the facts of what happened, but how we *remember* what happened, too."

Sera had to admit Dak had a point there. The SQ had proven there were a lot of ways they could mess with history. Sometimes, they didn't even need to change a particular event. All they had to do was get rid of certain books or change what was written about those events. So, yes, history was important, but that didn't mean she had to obsess over it the way he did.

"Sure, Dak," she said.

After that, Abi led them to another room he had prepared with more cushions and pillows and blankets.

"You'll sleep here," he said. "You must be tired."

Between their adventure in China, a whole day walking and running through the city, the big meal in her stomach, and the comfortable-looking bed in front of her, Sera was suddenly very tired.

"Get some rest," Abi said. "Hopefully, we will have news of Tusi in the morning."

They said good night, and he left.

Dak threw himself backward onto a pile of pillows. "I love this place."

Riq fell sideways onto a thick blanket. "I gotta say, it's pretty nice. I can't believe Hulagu's going to destroy it."

"He's not," Dak said. "We got this."

But something nagged at Sera. It had started when they were talking about history and books, and hadn't let up. She reached up to tug the hair that wasn't there anymore, a nervous habit left over from a time before she'd cut her hair short to disguise herself as a boy.

"What is it, dude?" Dak was looking at her. "You're pulling on air there. Something's bothering you."

Dak was right about that, in a couple of ways. There *was* something bothering her, something huge — she'd seen the Cataclysm. But that wasn't actually what she was thinking of at the moment.

"The SQ," she said. "We haven't identified a Time Warden here. They could be anywhere. They could be anyone. That just makes me nervous."

"The SQ will show themselves," Riq said. "They always do."

Abi woke them the next morning with a delicious breakfast of fruits and nuts, with more bread. "It is just as I suspected," he said as they ate. "Tusi is coming to the palace today."

"Will we go see him?" Sera asked.

"Yes, we leave shortly."

Sera was excited about the idea of meeting the great mathematician, someone she actually knew about for a change. She was certain he would help them, once he knew the situation. She didn't know how she would explain that situation, exactly, but she thought Abi would probably be able to do a better job than any of them.

They finished eating, and then Abi brought them some clothes to change into. Dak and Riq put on robes like most of the other men she'd seen. Sera put on a silk dress, with a beaded vest over a silk shirt with flowing sleeves. It was yet another dress, which she hated, but they all agreed they couldn't go before the caliph dressed in their Chinese clothing. After they'd changed, Abi led them from their room, back down the corridors of the House of Wisdom, around the central courtyard, and out the front door. He turned toward the palace they had seen the day before, and guided them to it.

As they drew closer, Sera's mouth hung open just a bit at the sight of it. The high walls, the domes, the towers. The palace guards admitted them through an imposing gate, after which they passed into a garden full of color. The plants here were obviously well cared for, and the air was heavy with floral fragrances. The scent of roses, in particular, struck Sera like a wave.

The dizzying fog of a Remnant fell over her, different from any she had ever felt before. Her past Remnants had always been vague, mostly feelings and impressions. But now, in this Remnant, she actually saw her mother. She was standing in a garden, pruning a white rosebush, a big, floppy hat on her head to keep the sun out of her eyes. She looked up, smiled, and beckoned for Sera to help her.

With that, the Remnant folded up and fluttered away, leaving Sera aching at what it had shown her. *Her mother.* Sera knew she had a mother now, out there somewhere. She wasn't going to let the Cataclysm take her away.

The Caliph

DAK NOTICED Sera rubbing her forehead. "Are you okay?" he asked.

"What?" She blinked and took a deep breath. "Yes, I'm okay."

"A Remnant?" Riq asked. "In the barn?"

Dak did a double take. Sera had told Riq about her parents' barn? It sounded like Riq knew more about what Sera experienced than Dak did, like the two of them had talked about it or something.

"No." She shook her head. "Let's — let's just keep going. I'm fine."

Riq looked worried, and so did Abi. Dak watched Sera, wishing he knew what Remnants were like, so he would know what she was going through. He didn't like Riq knowing things about his best friend that even Dak didn't know. But based on Riq's behavior, Dak guessed Riq must have Remnants, too. He wondered what those Remnants were.

"This way," Abi said.

They continued through the garden, and Dak heard a trumpeting sound up ahead.

"Is that" — Riq turned his head toward the noise — "an elephant?"

Abi nodded. "Yes, we are entering the Park of Wild Beasts."

They entered a new part of the garden where pens and enclosures lined the path. They saw giraffes and zebras and four elephants decked out in huge sheets of pink silk with silver embroidery. They passed cages rumbling with bears, lions, leopards, and tigers, some of which were led by chains held by what Dak assumed were very, very brave men.

"It's a zoo," Sera said.

"No, it's a *menagerie*," Dak said.

Riq lifted an eyebrow at him.

"What?" Dak said. "You're not the only one who knows words."

Riq chuckled and they moved on, past a large fountain, between two marble columns and into the palace. The floors were made of marble, too, carpeted by enormous rugs woven with many colors and intricate patterns of vines, flowers, and animals. Tapestries and silks hung from walls of stone and wood, which were covered in carvings. It all looked just how Dak had imagined it would when he'd read *One Thousand and One Nights*.

Guards patrolled the palace, but they didn't stop

Abi. He led the three of them through vast rooms, more courtyards, and into a second, inner garden. At the center of this garden was a shade tent, open on three sides. Near it stood a silver tree, with leaves of different colored metals. Jeweled birds of silver and gold perched throughout its branches, and they fluttered their wings and sang with the wind. Dak thought this must've been the kind of automata Abi had been talking about. Beneath the canopy, a man reclined on a sofa. His clothing was the fanciest Dak had seen so far, embroidered with golden threads, his turban made of a shiny material.

As soon as they'd taken a few steps into the garden, another man approached them. He was round, and he teetered toward them like a bowling pin. "What is the meaning of this, Abi?" he asked.

"Greetings, Grand Vizier," Abi said. "We have come hoping to speak with Tusi, once he has spoken with the caliph."

The vizier tipped his head sideways. "Is that so? What business do you have with Tusi?"

"It relates to the work of the House of Wisdom," Abi said. "Something the caliph fully supports."

"It is true the caliph has reverence and admiration for what you do. But as for whether you can speak with Tusi, you will have to ask the caliph yourself. You may approach him."

Abi bowed. "Thank you, Vizier."

Head bowed, he walked toward the man under the canopy. Dak imitated the gesture, and so did Sera and Riq. When Abi stopped at the edge of the tent, so did they. They waited a few moments as the vizier approached the man on the sofa, whom Dak assumed was the caliph, and whispered in his ear.

The caliph nodded and said, "You may approach, Abi."

Abi motioned with his hand for Dak, Sera, and Riq to stay where they were. He inched toward the caliph slowly, and when he was a few feet away, he said, "Peace, Commander of the Faithful, and may God's mercy be upon you." Then Abi lowered himself to his knees and kissed the ground.

As he did so, several servants came up and sprinkled Dak, Sera, and Riq with water, and then retreated. A moment later, Dak caught the smell, and realized the water was some kind of rose-scented perfume. He wrinkled his nose. Great. Now he smelled like *flowers*.

"Rise, Ibn Abī al-Shukr," the caliph said. "Tell me why you have come. My attendants say you've been asking about Tusi since yesterday."

"Yes, Caliph." Abi rose to his feet, but kept his head bowed. "I wish to speak with him about the fate of the House of Wisdom."

"What fate?" the caliph said. "And why would it matter to Tusi, the adviser to Hulagu Khan, the aggressor who sits outside our very gate?"

"Only this, Caliph. If we remind Tusi of the wealth of knowledge in the House of Wisdom, and in the whole city, perhaps he can persuade Hulagu Khan to spare the city the wanton destruction he has meted out against other cities before."

The caliph leaned forward. "Who are those children with you? And that young man?"

Dak looked up. The caliph was asking about them.

"Have them come forward," the caliph said.

Abi motioned them to approach. "They are students who have come from distant lands to learn at the House of Wisdom."

Dak swallowed. Did they need to kiss the ground like Abi had? He didn't know, but Sera and Riq didn't seem like they were going to, so he stayed on his feet, but still kept his head down.

"Who are you?" the caliph asked. "And why are you here with Abi?"

Riq spoke up first. "As Abi said, we are students from distant lands."

"What distant lands?" the caliph asked.

"Pennsylvania," Dak said.

"Pennsylvania?" The caliph scratched under his turban with his pointer finger. "I have never heard of this country."

"It's far away," Dak said. "Beyond . . ." He tried to think of a place. "Beyond Istanbul."

"Where?"

Oh, right, they haven't changed the name yet. "I mean, beyond Constantinople."

"I see," the caliph said.

The vizier was looking at Dak, Sera, and Riq like they had just sprouted tails or something, his expression stern.

"What do you study at the House of Wisdom?" the caliph asked.

"History," Dak said.

"Mathematics," Sera said.

"Linguistics," Riq said.

"Varied disciplines," the caliph said. "And what interest do you have in Tusi?"

"None," Riq said. "But as foreigners, we couldn't pass up the chance to come with Abi so we could see your famous palace."

That was a good answer, Dak had to admit.

"My palace?" the caliph said. "And what do you think of my palace?"

"It's amazing," Dak said.

"It's beautiful," Sera said.

"It's impressive," Riq said.

"It is all three of those things and more," Abi said.

"So it is," the caliph said. "And now, your request. What do you think, Vizier?"

The vizier frowned. "The caliph has nothing to fear from anyone. Tusi will try to persuade you to accept the terms of surrender you have already wisely rejected. Baghdad is completely safe, and therefore, so is the

House of Wisdom. Our women, alone, could defend the walls."

The caliph nodded. "Abi, I do not care whether you speak with Tusi or not, because it is irrelevant. You heard my vizier. We are perfectly safe from conquest."

Actually, thought Dak, *the exact opposite of that is true.*

"Go now," the caliph said. "I will have my vizier bring Tusi to you once I have rejected Hulagu's terms a second time."

"Actually," Dak said, "you might want to give those terms another look. The Mongols have been mostly undefeated in the expansion of their empire. When kings surrender to them, it usually goes okay for their people. But when kings *don't* surrender, bad things happen."

The caliph waved Dak off. "The Mongols shall suffer a rare defeat at Baghdad's gates."

Dak shook his head. "But—"

"Thank you, Caliph," Abi said. He backed away, and Dak did the same. So did Sera and Riq. Once they reached the edge of the tent, they turned and walked back toward the garden's entrance. The vizier came up behind them and waddled ahead.

"I will show you to a waiting room," he said.

They ended up in an open-air room surrounded by ornate arches and white marble columns. There were pillows and cushions on the ground, so they sat down and waited.

"He could just surrender," Dak said. "What I tried telling him was true. Hulagu spared lots of cities that surrendered. Cities that didn't surrender got pulverized. All you have to do is look at history so you don't repeat it."

"Let me guess," Riq said. "Now you're gonna tell us why history is so important and why you love it so much."

Dak felt his anger rising. "It's why *you* should love history instead of boring words, words, words."

"Stop it," Sera said. "Not in the palace."

Dak rolled his eyes. Riq was wrong, anyway. History was important, but that wasn't really why Dak loved it. He was still trying to figure that one out.

They waited quite a while. Dak was even starting to think he could close his eyes and take a nap. But then the vizier returned with a man who Dak assumed was Tusi. He wore a simple robe, with a white turban that wrapped around his head and dropped a tail of fabric down over his right shoulder. His beard was clean, smooth, and came to a point.

The vizier raised his voice a bit. "I present to you Nasir al-Din al-Tusi, emissary from Hulagu Khan." He took one last look at Dak and the others, scowling, and then he left.

Tusi waited, face blank, saying nothing.

Abi stepped forward. "I am Ibn Abī al-Shukr, and I am honored to meet you. Your reputation has spread far."

"And you have no reputation at all," Tusi said. "Why did you wish to speak with me?"

Wow, Dak thought. *That was rude.*

Abi blinked, seeming a bit taken aback. "I . . . certainly hope to one day have even a fraction of your learning and wisdom."

"Yes, yes," Tusi said. "Speak your mind so that I might be on my way."

Dak couldn't believe this guy.

"The caliph does not believe the city will fall," Abi said.

"No, he does not," Tusi said. "He is a fool."

"If the city does fall," Abi said, "I am worried that our libraries, and the House of Wisdom, will meet the same fate as those at Alamut fortress, where Hulagu captured you and destroyed the books there."

"He did not capture me," Tusi said. "He freed me from the Ismā 'īlī and allowed me to continue my work. Eventually, I became adviser to him."

"And that is why we hope you might persuade Hulagu to spare the libraries. Spare the House of Wisdom."

"No." Tusi didn't even act like he had given it half a thought.

"N-no?" Abi asked.

"No," Tusi said.

"Why not?" Riq asked.

Tusi turned to him. "Because my position with Hulagu is tenuous. It would take very little provocation for him to execute me, as he has done with countless others. I have therefore chosen not to provoke him. That is the best way to stay alive and continue my studies."

"So you won't speak for the libraries?" Sera asked.

"No," Tusi said. "I won't speak for anyone or anything but myself. If the libraries are destroyed, with all the books in them, I will grieve, secure in the knowledge that nothing could have been done."

"I don't understand," Abi said. "You are a scholar. You know what the House of Wisdom represents."

Tusi's eyes became sharp and narrow. "I know very well what it represents."

No one said anything. Dak couldn't believe this man, who had the power to maybe do something, but had refused to help. Where did that leave them?

"Is there anything more?" Tusi asked.

"No," Abi said.

Tusi nodded. "Then I bid you farewell." He turned and left.

After he had gone, Abi hung his head and shook it. "I don't understand," he repeated.

"What do we do now?" Dak asked.

"I don't know," Abi said.

"We come up with a new plan," Riq said. "We still have time."

"But I am troubled by something else," Abi said. "I think Tusi might be SQ. I think he *wants* the House of Wisdom destroyed."

The Mongol War Camp

RIQ THOUGHT about what Abi had just said. It made sense to him. If Tusi was really SQ, of course he wouldn't help save the House of Wisdom. He would want it destroyed. Maybe that was why he was advising Hulagu Khan in the first place. He was making sure the job got done.

"You think Tusi is SQ?" Dak asked.

"I do," Abi said. "I cannot think of another reason why a scholar such as he would refuse to help save the House of Wisdom."

"I think I agree with Abi," Riq said.

"Well, I don't." Sera folded her arms. "I can't believe that a man like Tusi would be SQ."

"Why not?" Dak asked. "You saw how rude that guy was."

"He may be rude," Sera said. "But he's also a mathematician and a scientist. I've learned about him. He is not SQ."

"The SQ has plenty of scientists," Riq said. "Tusi wouldn't be the first."

Sera appeared unconvinced.

"Either way, he's not on our side," Riq said. "Where does that leave us?"

"Well, we have to assume Tusi is SQ," Dak said. "And we *know* the caliph is an idiot. So I guess that means we have to go to Hulagu ourselves. Right?"

Riq thought about their options. His experience during the Viking siege of Paris, trapped within the city once the attack had begun, left him convinced that Dak's suggestion was the best idea left to them. "Right."

"This will be very dangerous," Abi said. "You will be venturing into the Mongol war camp."

Riq looked down at the robe he was wearing. He didn't want to walk into the Mongol camp while in Baghdad clothing. But then he remembered that Mongolia and China were next-door neighbors. "We might want to change back into our Chinese clothing so we don't look too out of place."

"That's true," Abi said. "And the Mongols have drawn soldiers from every nation and race they've conquered. You may be able to blend in. Let's hope that's enough to keep you safe."

They waited until nightfall, and Abi led them through the city streets, back through the Perfume Market, the stores all closed up and shuttered, then under the grand archway that stood before the mosque they had passed the day before. On the other side of the arch, they turned to the right and followed a wide street.

There were still a few people out, hurrying along. The windows and wooden screens above them to either side pulsed with the yellow flicker of candlelight and lamplight, and Riq heard the sounds of music, singing, and laughter coming from inside the houses and apartments. These people had no idea the Mongols were going to begin their siege the following day.

"The caliph has made them all feel safe when they're not," Riq said.

"That is true," Abi said.

The Hystorian kept them to the sides of the streets, in the shadows, and when he saw the city guards, patrolling with torches and lamps, he ducked the three time travelers into hiding places, down alleyways or behind street vendor stalls.

They came to a large intersection and turned left onto a new market street. The buildings here were larger and richer, almost like miniature palaces. Some distance on, Riq saw the city wall with a gate like the one they had first entered through the day before. But the gate was closed.

"How will we get out?" Riq asked Abi.

"We bribe the guards," Abi said. "Not the most elegant solution, but effective."

As they approached the gate, two guards stepped toward them and blocked their way.

"Greetings," Abi said.

"What business brings you to the Halbah Gate at this time of night?" one of the guards asked.

"Business with you," Abi said. "If you are interested in a transaction."

"What kind of transaction?"

"The simple kind," Abi said. "Money for a service."

"How much money?"

"A dinar between you," Abi said.

The guards paused. They looked at each other. "What's the service?"

Abi pointed ahead. "Open the gate and let my young friends pass."

The guards stared at them. Then one of them held out his open palm.

Abi reached into his robes and pulled out a coin. He placed it in the hand of the guard, who snatched it away. Riq flinched, hoping they would make good on their part of the bargain.

"The service?" Abi said.

The guard with the coin laughed through his nose. Then they both turned back to the gate, motioning for them to follow. They each pulled out a key, and unlocked a smaller door next to the larger city gate. The guards ushered them through, into an enclosed courtyard within the thick wall, to a second door.

"You're in the safest place you could be, right now," one of the guards said. "Why would you want to go out there? The Mongols are out there."

"We know," Riq said.

They shrugged and opened the door.

Abi looked at each of them. "Hulagu's war camp is due east. You won't be able to miss it. Good luck to you."

They said good-bye to him and stepped outside the city walls. The door shut behind them, and Riq heard the sound of the lock turning. The stars and moon overhead lit the desert around them with a cold, pale light. Riq could almost imagine the landscape was made of snow instead of sand.

"So, we just start walking?" Dak asked.

"Guess so," Sera said.

Riq noticed the flicker of campfires on the horizon, like someone had stretched out a string of carnival lights. "I think that's the war camp. Let's get going."

They set off across the sand, the chill of night around them.

"How far away do you think that is?" Dak asked.

"It's pretty close to the edge of our horizon," Sera said. "Which, given our height, would make it two to three miles away."

Riq picked up their pace. They had to get there as fast as they could. The siege would begin tomorrow.

Dak spouted facts about the Mongols on the way, and Riq just gritted his teeth and let the kid go. He explained that they were one of the most successful conquering empires in the history of the world, more or less undefeated in most of their battles. Often, they didn't even have to fight. Their enemies heard the Mongols were coming, and they just gave up. Some even believed that when the Mongols came, they were a divine punishment, so it was pointless to fight. Every single Mongol man was a warrior, and families traveled together on their military campaigns.

"That's why I don't understand what the caliph is doing," Dak said. "That vizier gave him the worst possible advice."

"It doesn't matter," Riq said. "What's done is done. We just have to stop Tusi."

"It's *not* Tusi," Sera said.

Riq just shook his head.

A few steps later, Dak piped up. "Did you know the Mongols tended to get hit by lightning a lot? There weren't any trees where they came from. Thunder terrified them."

Riq rolled his eyes. "Give it a rest, both of you."

They walked in silence after that, except for the scuff of their feet through the sand and the hiss of the wind. The emptiness of the desert left Riq time and room to think. And he didn't actually want to think right now. Any time he had a chance to think, his thoughts went to the future. Or his lack of future.

There was really only one thing Riq had thought of to do when the time came to return to the future. He couldn't risk traveling to an era where he'd be a complete anomaly. So he'd have to stay behind somewhere in the past, while Sera and Dak went back to the future to get their new SQuare. Then they could come back and pick him up to finish the remaining Great Breaks. He didn't know when he should tell them his plan, or how to convince them, but he'd have to do it soon.

"The desert is a little creepy," Dak said. "Like there's no one else in the world. It's like what the world would be after the Cataclysm."

"Don't talk about that." Sera's voice came out sounding sharp, almost angry.

Dak kept going. "I'm just saying—"

Sera stopped walking. "I said not to talk about it!"

"Geez, dude," Dak said, turning back to her. "Why don't you just tell us what's bothering you, already?"

"Nothing is bothering me," Sera said.

"Right," Dak said. "Just like nothing is bothering Riq."

Riq didn't say anything. He just kept walking.

"It's something to do with the Cataclysm," Dak said. "Obviously. So what is it?"

Sera resumed walking again, and Dak trotted to catch up.

"Well?" he said.

"It's . . ." Sera said.

Dak waited a minute. "It's what?"

Sera wiped at something in her eye.

"Are you crying?" Dak asked.

"I GOT SAND IN MY EYE!" Sera said. She'd obviously been pushed too far.

Dak's voice softened. "Sera, I didn't mean—"

"Leave it alone, Dak," Riq said. "She'll tell you when she's ready."

"Has she told *you*?" Dak asked.

Riq looked at Sera. They'd talked a bit about their Remnants back during the Viking siege of Paris. And here they were again. What was it about battles that brought this stuff up? Sera shook her head at Riq, telling him not to say anything.

Well, he sure didn't like being put in the middle of this.

"Dak, she'll tell *us* when she's ready." Which was the truth.

"You know what? I don't like secrets!" Dak said. "I need to know what's going on! It's like we're falling apart here, when we need to come together and be a team."

Riq had to admit the kid had a point. But he still wasn't ready to say anything about his own problems yet, and apparently Sera wasn't either.

"Let's just keep moving, Dak," Sera said. "Please?"

Dak folded his arms.

Sera touched his arm. "Please, Dak."

Dak relaxed his frown. "Fine. Okay. Let's go."

Riq was glad the two of them had worked it out, at least for now. They picked up their march again, the lights of the Mongol war camp pretty close now. Riq could see shadows moving in front of the campfires, silhouettes he couldn't quite make out. He heard dogs barking and horses neighing, and the clamor and ring of metal.

Once they reached the first few tents, Riq realized their plan was going to be a lot harder than he'd thought. The Mongol war camp was less like a camp and more like a mobile city. It was huge. And warriors stood armed and ready at every turn.

The Truth About Tusi

"IT'S ENORMOUS," Sera whispered. There were so many of the round tents, all arranged in a very orderly way. But what amazed Sera were the horses. They were everywhere. Lots of them. More than she could count. It seemed like the horses outnumbered the people five to one. Some of the horses had stuffed dummies mounted on them, as if the Mongols were trying to give the impression of more riders than they actually had.

"Let's look for Hulagu's tent," Dak said. "It will definitely stand out from the rest."

They snuck in between the tents, through the shadows, moving deeper and deeper into the Mongol territory. With each step, Sera had the feeling that this was the wrong way to go about saving the library. She didn't think there was any way they would be able to convince Hulagu Khan to do anything. It was ridiculous. She thought they should instead try to find Tusi.

She believed they could convince him somehow to help them. He was an amazing scientist, and he simply could not be SQ.

But no one had listened to her, even though she'd been right about a lot of things before.

The men in the Mongol army all wore the same uniform: a long wool coat that crossed in the front, buttoned under the right armpit, and was secured at the waist by a thin hide belt and wide sash. Leather armor was over that, to which scales and rings and other bits of metal had been attached. The women wore clothes pretty similar to the men, except without the armor, and some wore beaded, colored headdresses. They even wore pants like the men, which seemed practical for people who rode horses every day, and it made Sera smile.

The smoke of the fire and the smells of the food they cooked filled the air, and Sera saw that Abi had been right about the diversity in the Mongol empire. The three of them could pretty much fit right in. Their translation devices picked up a few different languages from the snippets of conversation they overheard.

They kept moving. And moving. All the tents started to look the same to Sera, and she wondered if they were going in circles.

"Guys," Sera said, "I'm just going to say one more time: I don't think Tusi is SQ."

"Oh, for the love of mincemeat," Dak said.

"We've been over this," Riq said.

Sera wanted to yell at them, but she tightened her lips and kept it inside.

More tents and more tents and more tents. And more horses.

"You wouldn't think they were going to battle tomorrow," Riq said. "Most everyone seems to be asleep."

"I think the Mongols slept pretty easy," Dak said. "They know how it's going to go down in Baghdad."

"What's that up there?" Riq nodded ahead.

An enormous white tent materialized out of the night sky, towering over the war camp. It seemed to be almost as big as a small baseball stadium. Sera figured that had to be Hulagu Khan's tent.

Now that they knew where they were going, the three of them hurried forward, but they hadn't gone far before Sera noticed the closer they got to the khan's tent, the more guards she saw posted, men wearing conical helmets with tufted points at the top, some with fringes of fur. Each of them had two swords, and some also had axes.

"We'll never be able to get close to Hulagu," Sera whispered.

Riq said, "Did you think he was going to send out an invite and roll out the red carpet?"

"No," Sera said. "I just don't know how we'll do this."

"I do," Dak said. "I know just the thing."

Sera recognized that tone. It was the tone Dak used

when he *thought* he knew just the thing, but hadn't stopped to actually think through that thing.

"Dak, stop and think first," Sera said.

Dak smiled. "I already did when I got the idea." He started forward, toward a group of guards.

"Dak!" Sera whispered. "Come back!"

But he was already too far away to hear her.

"That dumb kid," Riq said.

"Easy," Sera said. "He's still my best friend."

She and Riq watched as Dak strode right out of the shadows, swinging his arms wide in a high-footed march. Like he was *trying* to draw attention. The guards shouted a cry of alarm and swarmed him, weapons drawn.

"Oh, for the love of mi—" Riq stopped. "Was I seriously about to just say that?"

"Yup," Sera said.

Riq nodded. "Perfect. Just perfect. You stay here." He crept forward a few steps, and then marched out of the tents toward Dak and the guards. They instantly seized him, too. Sera strained forward to hear what they were saying, chewing on her lip, watching and waiting. She had no idea what Dak had planned here, but it made no sense to her.

After a few moments of questioning, the guards took hold of Dak's and Riq's arms and heaved them in the opposite direction of Hulagu's tent.

"No, wait!" Dak shouted. "We're spies! From Baghdad!

You need to take us before Hulagu! You were supposed to send us to Hulagu!"

So that had been his plan. But now they were taking him someplace else, a prisoner. Riq was shaking his head. He glanced in Sera's direction at one point, and gave a little nod, even though Sera knew he couldn't see her. It was all up to her now.

Sera was torn. Should she follow Dak and Riq and see where the Mongols were taking them, or should she go forward with the mission in the way she thought was best? If she did that, she would try to find Tusi.

In another moment, she would lose sight of Dak and Riq. She hesitated, and the moment she had to act was gone. They rounded a tent and disappeared. Sera felt a sickening hollow spreading in her stomach, but decided to hope they could take care of themselves. She would work on saving the House of Wisdom. Fixing the Break. *Saving her parents.*

Everything she did now was for them and to prevent the coming Cataclysm that would take them away from her.

She turned toward Hulagu's massive tent and crept forward. She actually had an easier time staying hidden without Dak and Riq. She was smaller and quieter than they were. The tent only got bigger as she got closer to it. When she finally had a view of the front entrance, with dozens of guards and horses, it confirmed to her that it would be impossible to get to Hulagu that way. Which was why her plan was better.

But how could she find Tusi? She figured he, as the khan's adviser, would probably have a nice tent, and it would probably be near Hulagu's. Sera started scouting around. There was a ring of tents around the khan's, and they were bigger and richer than the plain ones they'd seen since entering the camp. These were embroidered and painted. But none of them had any features that came right out and said, "Astronomer and mathematician inside."

It took quite a while, but Sera made it all the way around Hulagu's tent, sneaking past guards and regular Mongol warriors, without finding any sign. She was frustrated and discouraged. If Tusi was inside one of the tents nearby, she had no way of knowing. If he was somewhere else in the vast war camp, she had no way of finding him at all.

She kicked at the ground in frustration, and that's when she noticed something. There were markings in the dirt. Geometric markings with writing next to them. The writing looked like Arabic, but the markings were clearly diagrams. Specifically, two circles, one half the size and inside the other. It was the Tusi Couple. A bench leaned up against the tent right in front of the markings, and Sera could picture the whole scene:

Tusi, sitting on the bench, drawing in the dirt, working through problems. This tent had to be his. It had to be. Who else would have drawn these things?

She waited until the guards had passed, and then sneaked around to the tent entrance. With a deep breath, she stepped inside.

The inside of the tent was really comfortable. Thick rugs covered the floor in overlapping layers around a central wooden support post as thick as a small tree. Tapestries and silks hung from the sides of the tent, and tables around the room bore stacks of books and many brass instruments. In one area of the room, Sera saw a pile of cushions and pillows. When she focused on them, she realized there was someone sitting there, perfectly still, and she almost jumped.

It was Tusi. Staring at her.

"He-hello," she said. "I didn't see you there. Do you remember me?"

"Of course," Tusi said. "Why and how have you come here?"

"I came with my two friends," Sera said. "You met them. We came to convince you."

"Convince me of what?"

"To save the House of Wisdom."

Tusi sighed. He looked down at his lap, and Sera realized he had a book there, which he closed. Here he was with his books, stacks upon stacks of them, but he refused to do anything to save the books of Baghdad.

"Let me tell you something," he said.

Sera put her hands on her hips. "What?"

"After making me his adviser, Hulagu Khan came to me before this military campaign against Baghdad and asked me if the stars would smile favorably upon it. Now, I had a choice to make. I knew Hulagu *wanted* to attack Baghdad. If I had told him the stars were ill-favored, he may have spared the city for a time, but he would have been upset with *me*. He may have even executed me. But if I told him what he wanted to hear, that the stars were favorable to his ambitions, then he would be pleased with me."

"So you lied?"

"The movement of the stars is constant. However, the *interpretation* of those movements can be much more flexible."

Sera closed her eyes and shook her head. "That still just sounds like lying to me."

"You are young. When you are older, you will find that life is less absolute than you might wish it to be. There are few things you can truly rely upon other than the laws of the universe. And yourself."

Sera thought about that, and it sounded like a sad way to live. "I can rely on my friends. I can rely on my . . . *family*." As she said the word, its meaning shifted in her mind, gaining a new weight, a substance that included her parents in a way it never had before.

Tusi smiled. "If your friends and family be as constant as the movement of the stars, count yourself very lucky, indeed."

Sera walked over to the cushions and sat down. "The House of Wisdom contains many, many important books. They must be saved for future generations. Don't you see that?"

"Of course I see it. But there is nothing I can do."

"Hulagu Khan might listen to you."

"That's not a chance I am willing to take."

"Are you SQ?" She blurted out the question before she'd decided if she should.

"Am I what?" She saw no recognition of the name in his eyes. Just genuine confusion. If he had been SQ, he would have realized in that moment that she was a Hystorian, and things would have gotten a lot worse.

Sera sighed, vindicated. "Nothing. My mistake."

"What is your mistake?"

It was a mistake coming to you for help, she thought. But she said, "Nothing."

Tusi rose to his feet. "When the Ismā ʿīlī captured me and took me to their fortress at Alamut, I had a choice to make. I could resist and most likely perish, or I could adapt to them and continue my work. I chose to adapt and continue my work. When Hulagu Khan destroyed the fortress and freed me, I saw another opportunity. I could perish, or I could join him and continue my work. Again, I chose to continue my work."

He looked around his tent. "I continue it now, and I will continue it if every library in the world burns. The work is all that matters to me. My work. I can't let anything get in the way of that, so I cannot risk what you are asking of me. Do you understand?"

"I understand," Sera said. "You may not be SQ, but you're still not the man I thought you were."

10

The Divine Man

DAK'S IDEAS hadn't been turning out so well lately. He couldn't see what the problem was. They all seemed like good ideas when he first got them. But the trouble with ideas was that you often didn't know if they would turn out to be good until it was way too late to change them.

Like right now. Not a good idea to go walking up to Hulagu's guards asking to be arrested. Obviously. But now Dak and Riq were captured, and the Mongols were taking them in the opposite direction of where they needed to go.

"Sorry I got us into this," Dak said.

Riq shook his head. "I'll be sure to give you a hard time about it later. For now, we need to figure out what we're going to do."

"Sera will come for us," Dak said.

"Maybe. But we can't count on it. If she's smart, she's working on fixing the Break, not our mistakes." He paused, and then said very quietly, "The fate of the world is more important than any of our individual fates."

Okay, Dak *knew* there was something going on with the Cataclysm that these two weren't telling him. He hated that. He hated not knowing. He hated the uncertainty. It got his mind going, and then his fears, and soon his fears were outracing his thoughts. But he figured there wouldn't be any point asking Riq about it. Dak knew the guy didn't like him much, and wasn't about to open up.

"Where are you taking us?" Dak asked the Mongol warriors.

At first, they were silent.

"The Divine Man," one of the Mongols said at last.

"What does he mean?" Riq asked.

Dak shrugged. He had no idea. But when they arrived at a wide tent, he figured they were about to find out.

The Mongol warriors shoved them inside and pushed them to the ground. Dak looked around the tent. It was supported by four columns, and had numerous tables laid out with maps and charts. There was one sitting area, with cushions and pillows, but no rugs. This tent was a tent of war, not a tent of luxury.

A man looked up from the table he'd been leaning over and made eye contact with Dak. Dak immediately bowed his head. There was something about the man that provoked an instant fear. But Dak didn't like that, so he made himself look back up.

The man was not especially tall, but something about

him felt as strong and hard as a bronze statue. He came around the table, slowly, and stood in front of them, his hands clasped behind his back.

"I am General Guo Kan," he said.

"That's a Chinese name," Riq said. "You're working for the Mongols? I thought you were enemies."

"The great khan will accept anyone of ability, no matter how high or low one's birth, or one's nationality. Our army is full of men from all corners of the Earth. The engineers of our siege engines are the best minds in the world."

"Are you the Divine Man?" Dak asked.

"There are some who call me that."

"Why?" Riq asked.

"Because I have yet to be defeated in battle. Who are you?"

Dak didn't know what to say. What kind of lie could they tell that Guo Kan couldn't pick apart easily?

"We're just travelers," Riq said. "We arrived in Baghdad two days ago, and we decided to try to leave before the battle begins."

"But my men tell me you were asking to be brought before Hulagu Khan." The general made a slicing motion with his hand, some kind of order, and the men holding Dak began to rummage in his clothing, and squeeze his arms and legs, his torso. They were searching him, and of course they came up empty. "No weapons," Guo Kan said. "You weren't going to assassinate him. So why did you wish an audience with him?"

"We—" Riq faltered. "We're just travelers."

"Judging by your clothing, your language, and your demeanor, you must have come from very far away."

"We did," Riq said. "And we'd like to go now, if you don't mind."

Guo Kan looked up at his men. "Leave us. All of you."

Dak wondered what the general was doing. Why did he want everyone to leave?

When they were alone, Guo Kan smiled. "You don't know who I am. But I know who you are. Believe me when I tell you, the libraries of Baghdad will fall. There is nothing you can do to change the course of history."

Dak snapped upright. He looked at Riq, then up at Guo Kan. "You're SQ." Dak had walked himself and Riq right into the hands of the enemy.

"And you are Hystorians." Guo Kan smiled again. "Correction. You *were* Hystorians. Now where is the other one?"

"Other what?" Riq said.

"The girl."

Dak almost gasped. "Wh-what girl?"

"The girl my spies tell me you've been seen with."

"We don't know who you're talking about," Riq said.

"Really?" Guo Kan's eyebrows lifted in mock surprise. "The Market Inspector and the vizier know exactly who I'm talking about."

Dak's shock prevented him from saying anything in response. The Time Wardens had been aware of them almost from the beginning.

"Now that we've cleared that up," Guo Kan said, "I assume she has the device you use to travel in time."

"We lost that device." Dak lifted his hands and wiggled his fingers. "I'm pretty clumsy."

"You are also a miserable liar." Guo Kan called one of his men back inside. The warrior bowed, and Guo Kan said, "I want every tent in the camp searched for intruders before dawn. Get word out to the *tümen* commanders. Immediately."

"Yes, General," the man said, and left.

Dak swallowed, and worried about Sera. He didn't know where she was, but there was a good chance they'd find her.

"She's in the city," Riq said. "She didn't come with us."

"Of course she didn't." Guo Kan's gloating smile seemed to fill the tent. "If you are all the Hystorians have to send against us, the SQ has nothing to fear."

"Funny," Dak said. "The Time Wardens in the last eight places we've been all thought the same thing. Didn't turn out too well for them."

Guo Kan's smile shrank just a little. "Tides change."

"So does history," Riq said. "We've changed it."

"Not this time," Guo Kan said. "I am the Divine Man. I do not fail. And your failure here, now, will make all of your previous victories worthless."

His words stole the breath from Dak. Guo Kan was right. Failing just one mission would prove disastrous regardless of how much they'd accomplished. "Wh-what are you going to do with us?" Dak asked.

"For now, keep you here. I will find your friend and then I'll take the device and put an end to all three of you. In the meantime, I have a city to invade. And a library of Aristotle's books to destroy."

Dak and Riq sat on the ground, tied to one of the tent's support posts. They'd been left there for hours. Neither the guards nor Guo Kan had come back with Sera, and Dak chose to view that as a good thing. It meant she was still out there somewhere. Still free.

"I guess Sera was right," Riq said. "About Tusi."

"Guess so," Dak said. "But do we have to tell her that? We'll never live it down."

Riq chortled. "You're right. She'd milk that for all it's worth."

Dak laughed, too. "So what do we do, n−?"

"Shh." Riq cocked his head. "Do you hear that?"

Dak paid closer attention. He heard a rhythmic sound, a deep and pounding drumbeat. The noise of high-pitched howling and voices shouting. The thunder of horse hoofbeats. It almost felt like the ground shook beneath Dak where he sat.

"The Mongol army is on the move," Riq said. "It must

be dawn. The siege of Baghdad has begun."

"So we have to get back there," Dak said. "We have to get back into the city and find some other way to save the books."

"These ropes have a different idea about that."

"Well, what can we do about them?"

"I don't know," Riq said. "Wiggle?"

"Worth a try." Dak was aware of the fact that Riq was being sarcastic, as usual. But there didn't seem to be any other options. So for the next several minutes, the two twisted, shook, pulled, and worked at the knots, hoping they would start to loosen. But they almost seemed to tighten on the boys the more they tried to escape.

"Got any other ideas?" Dak asked.

"Nope. And why do I always have to come up with the ideas, anyway?"

"What do you mean? I have ideas!"

"Like the one that landed us here? Like telling a story about time travel in front of half the city? I meant *good* ideas, Dak."

Dak's face fell into a deep scowl. He knew not all of his ideas played out how he imagined. He knew he sometimes did things without thinking them all the way through. But wasn't doing something better than doing nothing?

"It always falls on me," Riq said. "That's how it's been this whole time. Well, one day, I might not be there for you two."

Dak was about to argue with the idea that Riq was the one who always managed to save the day, when the second part of what he'd just said really sunk in. "What do you mean, you might not be there?"

Riq was silent. He opened his mouth. Then he closed it. "Nothing."

Dak wondered if this had something to do with whatever had been bothering Riq. Something to do with his Remnants, or whatever it was. "No, really, what do you mean?"

"Just drop it."

"Fine. But don't say I didn't try."

"I won't."

"Good. And now I guess *I'll* have to come up with an idea. A *good* one." Dak looked up at the post where it joined with the top of the tent. He looked down at the foundation in the ground. It didn't seem to be buried or mounted to anything. "What if we both try to pull the same direction to move the bottom of the post?"

"We'll bring the tent down," Riq said. "And they'll know we're trying to escape. There're guards outside the door."

"Then we run."

Riq didn't say anything.

"We have to do something," Dak said.

Riq sighed. "Okay. Let's give it a try. Gently at first."

They shinnied their ropes up the post until they were both standing, and then they both pulled to the same side at the same time. The post lurched a little at the base.

"It's working," Riq said.

"I told you. Keep going."

"Just a bit at a time. We don't want to attract attention or bring the tent down until we're ready."

So for the next several minutes, they jerked and budged the base of the post a fraction of an inch at a time until it seemed like another tug or two would pop it free of the sand. The tent sagged a little, but so far no one had seemed to notice. Or at least, no one had come in.

"Okay," Riq said. "When the post comes free, we'll have to try really hard not to get tangled. We have to slide our ropes down off the post, and then somehow find our way out the entrance. Are you ready?"

"Ready," Dak said.

"On the count of three. One, two, three!"

They pulled hard together, the base of the post popped free, and the top of the tent folded and fell inward on them. It caught them both in the same hollow, the silk fabric rubbing the tops of their heads. Shouts sounded outside, the guards now fully alerted. Dak and Riq maneuvered the ropes, sliding them back down the post, until they came off the bottom, and without the post, the knots fell loose and away from their wrists.

The sounds of the guards shouting drew closer, burrowing into the tent, coming toward them.

"Okay," Dak said. "What now?"

"I don't know," Riq said. "This was *your* good idea!"

"Well, I don't know!" Dak said.

They heard a sudden tearing sound behind them as the tip of a knife rent the fabric. Another warrior, cutting his way in to find them? Dak could only watch as the knife worked its way down, opening up a large, tattered slit.

"You guys coming?" came a familiar voice from outside.

"Sera?" Dak poked his head through the opening, and there she was, standing over them, knife in hand. Dak scurried out, and Riq followed after him.

"Let's go," Riq said. "Before the guards figure out we've slipped out the back way."

The Mongol Siege

RIQ LED them back through the Mongol camp, which seemed deserted compared to the previous night. They raced between tents, dodging and weaving, trying to stay out of sight of the women and children and others who had stayed behind when the army had marched out. Riq listened for sounds of pursuit behind them, but heard none. When they reached the edge of the camp, he saw a cloud of dust and sand ahead of them, kicked up by the riding army, rising up into the air over Baghdad.

"So, just for clarification," Sera said, "we're trying to find our way through that battlefield, and somehow get back inside the city to figure out a new plan to save the House of Wisdom, right?"

"Right!" Dak said.

"Easy," said Riq with a wry smile.

"You were right about Tusi," Dak said to Sera. "He's not SQ."

"I know," Sera said.

"Well, you don't have to be cocky about it," Dak said. "You didn't *really* know until I just told you."

"No, I know because I asked him last night."

"You did?" Dak asked.

"Yes."

"You found him?" Riq asked.

"I did." Sera shook her head. "He hid me when the camp was being searched. And then he told me where to find you two. But he still won't help us save the library. Which means he might as well be SQ, even if he isn't."

"Well, that's that," Riq said. "We'll make a new plan with Abi." He started off across the desert sand. "The good news is that we're moving *with* the Mongol army. Less likely to get trampled by their horses that way."

"Thanks for that," Dak said. "But you should know the Mongols were famous for being able to shoot their bows in any direction *while* galloping on their horses, with deadly accuracy. Even backward. Which is where we'll be coming from."

"Thanks for *that*," Sera said.

"They'll be focused on the city," Riq said. At least, that was what he hoped.

They trudged across the miles of sand between the war camp and the city, getting steadily closer. Baghdad waited ahead, appearing helpless and small, while the Mongol army seemed to stretch from one edge of the horizon to the other, completely surrounding the city walls. The bulk of the army's movement and forces seemed to be concentrated straight ahead of them on a part of the wall with a massive tower.

Riq didn't think the three of them would be able to get anywhere near the gates on this side of Baghdad. They'd have to circle around and use the river to get to the House of Wisdom.

By the time they reached the Mongol army, the warriors had assumed their formations. The sights and smells presented a vivid reminder to Riq of the Viking army back in Paris, but the Mongols appeared much more disciplined and organized. The sound of their assault was deafening.

The bulk of the cavalry hung back at the rear, while before them the Mongol siege engines had begun to pound the city. Catapults hurled huge rocks at Baghdad's walls, and giant crossbows fired burning bolts right over them. Riq could only imagine the fear and destruction that must be raging through the streets inside. It was obvious that the city couldn't last long under such an attack.

In front of the siege engines, Mongol archers raced forward on horseback, galloped along the walls, firing arrow after arrow up at the city's soldiers, and then retreated behind the line. The bravery and skill of their maneuvers were pretty amazing.

The three of them crept along behind all the action, unnoticed, or at least ignored.

"We'll swing around to the other side of the city," Riq said. "Then we'll use a boat to make our way down the river to the Wharf of the Needle-Makers. Sound good?"

"Sounds good," Sera said.

"Lead on," Dak said.

So they swung around behind the army, under the desert sun, as all along Baghdad's walls, the Mongols maintained a constant barrage. It took quite some time for them to even see the river away to the northwest, but when they did, Riq had sudden doubts about his plan.

Mongol forces lined the shore thickly enough that he worried they wouldn't be able to reach the river.

"We'll just have to sneak past them onto a boat," Sera said.

Riq turned to Dak. Here was a rare moment when his knowing something about history might actually be useful. "How long did the siege last?" he asked.

"Seven days," Dak said. "Then the Mongols took over that big tower we saw, called the Persian Tower."

"Then we have a little time. I think we should hide out and try to cross the river at night," Riq said. "We'll be more likely to sneak past them that way."

So they hunkered down in a shallow wash and waited for night to fall. The sun passed overhead, and the hours ticked by. It didn't take long for Riq to feel the effects of not having any food or water. His lips and throat got dry. Hunger gnawed at his insides. The physical discomfort added to his fear and dread about what the future held for him.

He'd been close to telling Dak about it back in Guo Kan's tent, but in the end he couldn't bring himself to do it. It was like he was afraid to say it out loud. Like that would make it more real somehow. He was also unsure of *how* to say it. For all the languages he knew, sometimes it was still hard to find the right words for some things.

"Do you wonder what's going on in the future?" Dak asked. "What the world looks like with the Breaks we've fixed?"

Riq froze at the question. He noticed Sera did, too.

"Like the first Break. I bet there's a lot of stuff named after Columbus now." Dak traced his finger in the sand, a zigzag, like he was connecting invisible dots. "I bet French history is pretty different since the SQ weren't able to stop the Revolution. It's, like, nothing is settled. Everything is up in the air. Everything we're doing is making changes."

"You seem a little bothered by that," Sera said. "Isn't that the point of what we're doing here?"

"I guess," Dak said.

"You guess?" Sera asked.

"I mean yes," Dak said. "Of course that's the point. It's just . . ."

"Just what?" Riq asked.

Dak frowned. "History is supposed to be settled."

"It will be," Riq said. "When we're finished with the mission, it will be settled once and for all."

They waited until the sun had gone down completely, and the sky was a deep black all the way across. The sounds of battle had faded in the darkness, but fires all along the front lines showed the Mongols were still there, waiting to resume their full assault with the dawn. By moonlight, Riq, Sera, and Dak scurried toward the river.

They aimed for a dark, empty spot between two campfires, around which warriors sat and slept. Riq hoped that with the light in their eyes, the Mongols wouldn't be able to see too far into the shadows. The time travelers slipped down to the river's edge in single file, where the moon glistened over the inky water, and the sound of it lapping the shore hid some of the sounds they made.

A cluster of small boats rocked gently with the current, bumping into one another and against the small dock to which they were tied. The three of them waded into the river toward them, the water chilly against Riq's skin. Dak went to the ropes securing the boats, while Sera climbed into one and kept herself low.

"I'm going to let them all loose," Dak whispered. "That way, they won't have a boat nearby to follow us, and they won't know which one we're in."

"Good idea," Riq whispered back. Apparently, the kid did have them on occasion.

Once the ships were floating free, Dak gave them each a push out into the river, where the current grabbed them and pulled them away. Riq held on to Sera's boat, and once Dak had climbed into it, Riq heaved it out into the river and scrambled on board after them.

"Well," Sera said, "that went we—"

A cry of alarm sounded on the bank.

Riq turned back to see shadows racing from the campfires down to the shoreline.

"Do you think they can see us?" Dak asked.

Something hissed and splashed in the water near the ship. An arrow.

"I'd say so," Riq said. "Quick, grab the oars!"

They swung the paddles out over the water and plowed ahead as fast as they could. More arrows flew at them, striking the water, a couple of them even hitting the hull of the ship.

"We got lucky," Dak said. "I don't think they can see us very well."

"They can see well enough," Riq said.

They paddled ferociously until their boat was out of range of the archers, but Riq didn't feel like they could let up. They had to reach the Wharf of the Needle-Makers quickly in case the Mongols decided to round up some other boats and come after them.

They moved down the river, and before long, the

buildings of Baghdad stood to either side. The city lights reflected toward them in wavering strips along the river. The caliph's palace soon came into view, and Riq steered the craft toward the shoreline near it.

They came up to the Wharf of the Needle-Makers, and above it Riq saw the House of Wisdom. He relaxed a bit and breathed a sigh of relief, a little amazed they had made it back into the city from the Mongol war camp. They pulled up alongside the pier, and Dak jumped out. He tied the boat off, and then helped Sera up. Riq followed after him, but before he'd quite gained his footing, someone shouted.

"Halt!"

Riq turned as half a dozen of the city guards approached them, swords drawn.

"Spies!" one of the guards shouted.

Riq held up his hands. "We're not spies. We're visiting scholars at the House of Wisdom. We're your allies."

The guards surrounded them, still brandishing their weapons.

"What proof do you have?" one of the guards asked.

"Seriously?" Dak said. "Just go get Abi and he'll tell you."

"You're friends of the traitor Abi?" the guard asked. "Then I have a better idea. We'll take you to the grand vizier, and let him decide what to do with you."

"Traitor?" Dak asked.

"Great!" Sera said. "Take us to the vizier."

Riq opened his eyes wide and stared at her. "No, not great!"

"Why?" Sera asked. "The vizier knows who we are. He can vouch for us."

"No," Dak said. "You don't get it. Hulagu's general Guo Kan is a Time Warden, and he told us about his spies in the city. The vizier is SQ!"

Imprisoned

THE GUARDS marched Sera, Dak, and Riq up from the river toward the palace. Knowing the SQ had agents both outside *and* inside the city made the situation seem that much more hopeless. But Sera refused to give up. She couldn't. They had to fix the Break no matter what.

"At least we know why the vizier gave the caliph such bad advice," Dak said. "He was working from the inside to make sure Baghdad gets destroyed."

"Yes," Riq said. "And that makes me feel so much better about being his prisoner."

They entered a smaller building near the palace. It had thick walls and very narrow windows. The guards pushed the three of them ahead, down a hallway, into one of several cells. Metal squealed as the guards swung the iron bars shut on them and locked the door, then left without another word.

"So this isn't good," Sera said.

"Hystorians?" The voice came from across the hallway in the cell opposite theirs. Abi stepped forward from the shadows. "Is that you?"

"Yes!" Sera felt relieved to see him again, even here. "Are you all right, Abi?"

"I am unharmed," he said. "They arrested me shortly after I helped you get out of the city. Were you able to convince Hulagu to spare the libraries?"

"We never even saw him," Dak said. "Riq and I got caught by General Guo Kan, who's a Time Warden, by the way. Sera tried one more time to convince Tusi, but he wouldn't listen to her."

Abi hung his head, and the broad smile he normally wore fell from his face. "Then it seems we have lost hope."

"Please don't say that." Sera had to fight pretty desperately within herself to keep from feeling the same way. There had to be another option. Something they hadn't thought of. If she still had her long hair, she'd be pulling it clean out right now as she studied the bars and their cell for a way to escape.

"It's okay," Riq said. "We'll think of something."

"Right," Dak said. "This isn't the first cell we've been locked in."

Sera took a deep breath. Then she grabbed hold of the bars and tested them one by one to see if any of them were loose. They weren't. She went to the narrow window and peered outside. Their cell wasn't up high, so there wasn't a fall to worry about on the other side. The window was just too small. But the mud bricks were soft enough that they might be able to chip away at them if they had some kind of tool.

"Do any of you have anything on you?" she asked.

All the three of them had with them were the Infinity Ring and the SQuare. But from deep within his robes, Abi pulled out a small knife.

"They missed this when they arrested me," he said. "I keep it on me for sharpening quills. It's useless for anything more than that."

"Maybe not," Sera said. "Can you toss it over?"

Abi approached his bars and stuck his arm through them. "Watch out. Here it comes."

He lobbed the knife gently into the air, and it sailed toward them. But it clanged against their cell door and bounced back into the middle of the hallway.

Sera rushed up to the door with Dak and Riq. Abi's arm still hung through his own cell's bars. They all stared at the knife on the ground between them.

"I'm a scholar, not an athlete," Abi said. "I never could throw well."

Riq dropped to the ground. "My arms are the longest." He reached through the bars, along the ground, straining to reach the knife. The tip of his middle finger almost touched it, but not quite. He grunted and pushed but couldn't get close enough. Finally, he stood, dusting himself off. "I can't."

Sera looked around again, this time with an eye toward anything that might help them reach the blade.

They had nothing. She glanced across the hallway at Abi, who looked completely defeated, resting his turbaned head against the bars.

His turban!

"Abi!" she said. "How long is your turban?"

Abi lifted his head. "Several cubits. Why?"

"If we stretch it between us, and then drag it along the floor, we might be able to snag the knife and pull it closer."

Abi seemed reluctant at first, but eventually sighed, closed his eyes, and reached up to his turban. He began uncoiling it from his head, a process that took some time and showed how intricate the headpiece was in the first place. Beneath the turban, his dark hair was long, and he wore it braided.

"I'll try to do better this time." He held one end of the fabric in one hand, and bunched up the rest of it in the other. He tossed the bunched end toward Sera, and it unraveled through the air toward her, landing safely within reach. They lowered it to the ground, pulled it tight between their cells, and held it against the ground over the knife. Then Sera pulled it toward her. The knife didn't move, so she let Abi pull some fabric back and they tried it again. And again.

Finally, the tip of the knife caught in the weave of the fabric, and as Sera pulled, it pivoted the knife to a standing position, the blade pointing up. She pulled some more, and the knife came down.

"I can reach that now," Riq said.

He dropped to the ground as Abi pulled his turban back and began rewrapping it around his head. Then the sound of a door opening came from down the hallway.

"Hurry!" Dak whispered. "Someone's coming."

Riq reached through the bars, the knife just barely within reach of his fingertips. He swiped at the blade.

"Careful," Abi said. "It's sharp."

"I know," Riq said, grunting.

Sera heard footsteps just around the corner.

"Riq," she whispered.

"Got it!" He whipped his arm back into the cell, the knife in his hand, just as two guards came into view. The grand vizier wobbled between them.

"So, you three" — he cleared his throat — "*scholars* have come back to join the traitor?"

"I am no traitor," Abi said. "It is you who have promoted a disastrous course of action with the caliph for your own gain."

"It's more than that," Dak said. "He's SQ."

Abi blinked. "What?"

"Yeah," Riq said. Sera noted he had already hidden the knife out of view. "So is the Market Inspector. They're working for Hulagu's general Guo Kan."

"I see." Abi's normally soft expression had become suddenly hard and angry.

The grand vizier sneered. "You see nothing. For all the books in your House of Wisdom, you are not very wise." He turned toward Sera, Dak, and Riq. "And now give me the device."

Sera folded her arms.

The vizier raised his voice. "Do not make it necessary for me to kill any of you! Hand over the device!"

Sera looked at Dak and Riq, she looked at Abi, and she couldn't imagine letting anything happen to any of them when she could do something to prevent it. She reached into her coat and pulled out the Infinity Ring.

The vizier held out his hand. "Give it to me."

Sera clenched her jaw. She slowly passed the Ring between the bars. The vizier took hold of the other end, and for a moment they played a silent game of tug-of-war before Sera allowed her fingers to relax and let it go.

The vizier tucked the Ring inside his robes. "You will remain locked in here until the House of Wisdom falls. After that, you will be released, and it matters not what you do."

It wouldn't matter because they would be stranded in the ancient Middle East. Sera wondered if she'd made a mistake handing the Ring over so easily, but she also knew there wasn't much else she could have done. She'd bought them some time, at least.

The vizier turned with his guards and marched away. No one said anything. They all seemed to be listening to the fading sounds of footsteps. When it was silent, Dak threw up his hands.

"Well, that's just great."

"It'll be fine," Sera said. "We'll just have to find a way to get the Ring back after we save the House of Wisdom."

"Which we still don't know how to do," Riq said.

"Well, the first step is to get out of this cell," Sera said. "You have the knife?"

"Yeah." Riq pulled it out. "What are you thinking?"

Sera pointed at the window. "We chip away at the bricks until we can break a few of them free and we climb out."

"What about Abi?" Dak whispered. "He can't escape through our window. We can't just leave him."

Sera hadn't thought about that.

"What about picking the lock?" Dak asked.

"Right," Riq said. "Have you ever picked an ancient Baghdad lock before?"

"No," Dak said. "But how complicated can it be?"

"Quite complicated," Abi said from his cell. "But not impossible."

"Do you know how?" Dak asked.

"I know how the mechanism works," Abi said. "But we'll need more than a knife. We also need a pick of some kind."

Sera had already taken inventory of what they had available in the cell. There was only one thing left, and it made her feel queasy to think about it. She reached into her coat and pulled out the SQuare. The vizier didn't know to ask for it, so she'd managed to hang on to it.

She spoke hesitantly. "I could probably take this apart and make something to use."

"The SQuare?" Riq's eyes grew wide. He seemed afraid of something.

Dak nodded. "Why not? We were going to have to go to the future to get a new one, anyway."

"And I'll try to put it back together when I'm done." Sera wasn't sure why Riq looked so frightened. "It'll be okay."

Riq took several deep breaths. "Okay. Okay, do it. The mission is what counts."

Sera sat down with the SQuare in her lap. There was a seam between the screen and the metal body. She took the blade of the knife and teased it into the seam, then slipped the knife around the entire edge of the SQuare, breaking the seal. Then she popped the screen off, splitting the SQuare open like a clam's shell.

Dust and debris filled the cracks and hollows inside the device, covering some of the circuitry and the battery. All their adventures until now had apparently been taking their toll, and Sera felt guilty for having neglected the device. The particles that had found their way into the SQuare had come from eight different times in history and almost as many locations from all around the world.

"It really needed to be cleaned, anyway." Sera inhaled and tried her best to blow the dust away. "I can't believe I let it go this long. I clean the inside of my phone more often than this."

"You clean the inside of your phone?" Riq asked.

"Are you kidding?" Dak said. "She cleans the inside of her *calculator.*"

Sera felt her face flushing. "So? What about it?"

"Nothing." Riq was hiding a smile, Sera could tell.

"For the love of mincemeat," Sera said, "I can't help it if I'm the only one who knows about the proper care of electronics. Dust is death, you know." She blew on the SQuare again. "And I can't believe this thing is still going."

"It was made to last the whole mission," Riq said.

"Not the *whole* mission," Dak said. "Can we use anything in there?"

Sera scanned the components. Most of it was pretty much what she expected. There were a few surprises in the placement of things, but overall it was a pretty well-made device. She immediately saw some metal brackets that she could pull out. Even if she couldn't get them back in afterward, the SQuare would work without them, as long as it didn't get bumped around too badly.

"Yes," she said. "I think we're in business."

Silk and Locks

DAK WINCED a little as Sera ripped some thin pieces of metal from the SQuare. But Riq looked like he felt actual physical pain at seeing the device gutted. Sera pressed the two halves back together and slipped them back into her coat. She held out the metal strips.

"Who wants to try?"

Dak laced his fingers and cracked his knuckles. "I'll give it a shot."

Sera handed him the knife and the metal pieces. He walked to the door. Abi stood across the way, nodding.

"All right," the Hystorian said, "there are pins inside you must lift with those picks, and then turn the lock with the knife."

Dak knelt down. "Okay." He took the metal pick in one hand, and the knife in the other. "You sure you don't want to take a crack at yours first?"

"Your fingers are far more nimble than mine. Start by exploring with those picks. Listen to the sounds inside the lock. Feel what's going on inside it."

Dak reached his arm around through the bars and slipped the pick inside the keyhole. He poked around, exploring, forming an image in his mind of what the inside of the lock looked like. He thought he could tell where the pins were. He experimented with pushing on them, figuring out how they moved, and when he thought he was ready, he stuck the tip of the knife in the lock and tried to lift the pins and turn the lock at the same time.

It was not easy.

In fact, it was hard. *Really* hard.

His impatience and frustration got the better of him. The pieces were just so tiny, and he couldn't get them to work right. He jumped to his feet with a growl. "Someone else take a turn."

"You're doing well," Sera said. "You were figuring it out. Keep trying."

Dak frowned. Maybe they should try chipping away at the window like Sera had suggested, after all. Dak walked over to it and looked outside. He noticed that during his lock-picking attempts, the sun had started to rise. The pink dawn light and the blue shadows it cast fell on the clay walls and buildings around them. Within moments, Dak heard what sounded like thunder. But he recognized the noise for what it was.

"The Mongols have started up their siege again," he said. "Day two. Five more to go."

"Then what happens?" Riq asked.

"Well . . ." Dak resisted the urge to point out how useful historical facts could be. He'd been resisting saying a lot of things like that the past few days. He was trying hard to be nice, even though it was really starting to bother him that he didn't know what was going on with Sera and Riq. "After that, Hulagu moved into the city. He set up his own temporary palace. Five days after that, the caliph surrendered, and the Mongols went through the city, destroying everything."

"So we better get this door open," Sera said.

Dak sighed. Some of the frustration he'd been feeling had faded a bit. "Okay, I'll keep trying."

He went back to the lock, and was about to kneel down, when the sounds of footsteps approached again from down the hallway.

"They're coming back!" Dak backed away from the door, and shoved the knife and pick inside his coat.

Two guards came into view holding some clay bowls. They unlocked the door to Dak, Sera, and Riq's cell and opened it just wide enough to push the bowls inside, along with a pitcher of water. They did the same with Abi's cell.

"Food," one of the guards said, even though that was obvious. They relocked the doors and left.

One bowl had some kind of beans in it. They were mushy and tasteless. The other bowl had some kind of oatmeal or something. There weren't any utensils, so they just took turns eating with their dirty fingers. It was pretty gross, but Dak was hungry enough that he didn't care.

After he'd finished eating, he went back to the lock, but still couldn't get it. He passed the knife and pick off to Riq. "You try. I can't."

But Riq couldn't either. And neither could Sera. After a full day of trying, Dak realized that even if Abi said it was "not impossible" to pick the lock, that didn't mean it was likely.

"I think we need to go back to busting out the window," Dak said. "But it'll take a while, and I don't know how we'll do it with the guards dropping in on us."

"We need to wait and see when they come back," Riq said. "Once we figure out their pattern, we'll know when we stand the best chance."

"That still doesn't solve the problem of leaving Abi behind," Sera said.

Oh, right. Dak turned to look at the scholar.

Abi shook his head. "Young Hystorians, you must fix the Break. Do not worry about me."

That didn't sit well with Dak, but right now, they didn't seem to have any other options. So they settled in to wait for the guards to return. While they waited, Sera tried to put the pieces back into the SQuare, but all the lock-picking attempts had apparently taken their toll.

"I can't get them back in," Sera said.

"So what does that mean?" Riq's voice had an edge of panic.

"Maybe nothing," Sera said. "They were just brackets

holding things in place. It will still work. For a while."

"For a while?" Riq asked.

"Probably for as long as we need it to," Sera said. "Things are just a little loose inside."

Dak watched Riq's reaction, and started trying to put things together. The guy was really worried about the SQuare breaking. But Dak didn't get that, because they had to go back to get a new one, anyway. But now that Dak thought about it, he realized Riq had been acting weird ever since they'd gotten that message from Brint and Mari. Was Riq worried about going back to the present? Why? The only thing Dak could come up with was that it had something to do with his Remnants.

Remnants. It had all started with Aristotle's Remnants, and it always seemed to come back to Remnants. Even though Dak wished he knew what they were like for Sera, he was mostly grateful he didn't have Remnants. They didn't seem to bring anyone anything but pain. And fear.

But having actual parents missing in time was worse. Dak hadn't yet seen a sign of his parents in this era. He'd been trying really hard not to think about it, but he couldn't help wonder if that meant something. Maybe Dak, Sera, and Riq had fixed enough Breaks that his parents had gone home. Would they be there in the future when he went back for a new SQuare?

His heart started beating faster at that thought. It

filled him with hope, even as the sounds of battle raged on outside.

The guards came back that evening with a second meal that consisted of the same stuff as the first meal. They dropped off the food and water, took away the empty bowls from earlier, and left.

"I don't think they'll be back until morning," Riq said. "Now is probably our best chance if we're going to try and chip our way out of here."

He took out the knife and went over to the window. Dak watched as Riq ran the blade along the edges of the mud bricks and scraped at their seams. He tried to drive the knife in between them, putting all his weight behind it.

"They're harder than they look," he said. "This is going to take a long time. Too long." But he went back to it, and soon he'd worked up a sweat, even though the sun had set and the room was getting colder as it got darker.

The third day of siege had come to an end. They were running out of time. Dak's thoughts went to the unstoppable Mongol army, and facts started bubbling in his head. Normally, each fact just kind of popped and went away, replaced by the next, but right now, one of them was staying around.

The Mongols did something cool with their armor. They wore silk underneath it, against their skin. When an arrow pierced their armor, the arrowhead got caught in the silk, and even if it then pierced the warrior's skin, the silk made the arrow easy to pull out, and kept the injury cleaner and less deadly.

Dak kept thinking and thinking about this fact. There was something about it that seemed to apply to this situation. He turned his attention from Riq's attempts to chisel at the window and looked around the cell. He looked at the door. The lock where he'd spent several frustrated hours.

The lock.

That was it! Dak almost wanted to jump. "Abi!"

Sera and Riq startled in surprise at his outburst.

"Yes?" Abi said.

"Can I cut off a piece of silk from your turban?" Dak asked.

"I . . . I suppose if it is absolutely necessary." Abi started unwinding it from his head again. "What do you plan to do?"

"You'll see," Dak said.

A few moments later, Abi tossed one end of the thin fabric across the hallway, and Dak used the knife to slice off a couple of inches. Abi pulled the rest back, while Dak took the metal pick that Sera hadn't been able to put back in the SQuare. He went to the door, reached around, and laid the piece of silk from Abi's turban over the keyhole. Then he took the pick, and gently packed the silk into the lock. He remembered the way the inside looked in his head, and he packed the silk all around the pins.

"What are you doing?" Sera asked.

"The silk is quiet," Dak said. "And slippery. When the guards go to use their key, I think the silk will give enough to let the door unlock, but then it'll jam up the pins, and keep it from locking again when they close the door. We'll be able to walk right out of here."

"Uh, don't you think the guards will notice the door not staying shut?" Riq asked.

"Not if we do something to keep them from noticing," Dak said. "And I've got an idea for that, too."

Dak explained it to them, and they were both quiet. So was Abi.

"Dak?" Sera finally said.

"Yes?"

"I think this might be one of your *good* ideas."

Dak smiled with a bit of pride. "Let's hope it works."

The rest of that night, they rehearsed what they would do when the guards came. Riq tossed the knife and pick to Abi, managing to land them both right through the bars, and Abi cut some silk and did the same thing with the lock on his door.

The sun came up, and everyone waited without saying much. Then, sometime midmorning, Dak heard the guards coming. He nodded to Riq and Sera. They nodded back.

Moments later, the guards came into view with the

same bowls of nasty food. One of them pulled out his key and stuck it into the lock. Dak's heartbeat quickened. He held his breath. The guard tried to turn the key, stopped, and looked down at the lock.

Was it going to work?

The guard turned harder, and the lock clicked. He pulled the key out and opened the door the same foot or so they always did to slide the bowls of food in and out.

Dak readied himself, and hoped Riq was doing the same.

Then, right as the guard went to close the door, Dak launched himself at it.

Jailbreak

"NO!" DAK screamed. "Let me out! You can't keep me here!"

Riq rushed the door, too, ready to play his part. The guard reacted to Dak's charge by slamming the door shut hard just as Dak crashed against it. Dak and Riq grabbed the bars at the same time, and while Dak made a show of tugging hard on them, Riq used his strength to keep the door from opening. Assuming the door would open.

The guards stepped away from Dak's thrashing at the door. "Back off!" one of them shouted.

Dak stopped pulling and glared at them.

"Back off," the guard said again.

Dak stepped away from the door.

"You want to eat," the guard said, "you won't ever try anything like that again. Understand?"

"I understand," Dak said.

The guards turned to Abi. They unlocked his cell, and

as they went to close it again, he performed a variation of what Dak had done, though not quite as extreme. The guards did not look pleased.

"You, too, traitor?" one of them said. "Just for that, no food for any of you tonight! This is all you get until tomorrow."

"You can't do that!" Sera shouted.

"No?" The guard looked at her. "I guess you'll find out when you go to sleep hungry tonight."

Sera let out a little whimper that Riq would have believed completely if he didn't know her better. Sera just wasn't the whimpering type.

The guards gave them all one last glare and stalked away. Everyone waited until they were long gone, the hallways completely silent, before they approached the door.

"Moment of truth," Riq said. He had to admit, if this worked, it would be one of Dak's finest moments. So he decided to let the kid have it. "Why don't you try the door?"

Dak took a deep breath and stepped forward. He grabbed the bars and gave a gentle tug. Nothing happened. Dak closed his eyes and pulled again, harder, and the door popped open. Riq stared at it, not quite sure he could believe what he was seeing.

"You did it!" Sera actually giggled.

Dak smirked in that cocky way that Riq had found so annoying from day one. "Of course I did."

That changed Riq's mind about the compliment he

had been about to give. He turned to Abi. "Did it work for your door?"

Abi pulled on the bars, and his door also popped open. "Yes," the Hystorian said with a smile.

The four of them left their cells and looked down the hallway. Riq had no idea where the guards were, but he was pretty sure he remembered how to get from their cells back to the front door.

"Follow me," he said. "Quietly."

He led them down the hallway and around a couple of turns, each time listening carefully before peering around the corner. The place was deserted. The guards weren't anywhere to be seen.

"Looks like nobody comes here," Riq said. "I bet the vizier picked this place so we wouldn't be discovered. The guards don't even seem to stick around except to bring us our food."

"I hope they left the front door open," Dak said.

It turned out that they had. The front door didn't even lock.

"Okay," Riq said. "Before we go out there, what's the plan?"

"In three days Hulagu will be inside the city walls," Dak said. "I say we try to meet him there and do what we were going to do in the war camp. What we've been trying to do from the beginning. We convince him to spare the House of Wisdom."

"What about the Infinity Ring?" Sera asked.

Riq considered what to do. Guo Kan had said the vizier worked for him. That meant the vizier was probably going to turn the Ring over to the general the first chance he got. Once the general got ahold of it, Riq was pretty sure the Ring would disappear for good. So they had to get it back before Hulagu and Guo Kan entered the city.

"I think we need to split up," Riq said. "Two of us try to get to Hulagu, while the other two go after the Ring. We meet back at the House of Wisdom."

"Okay," Dak said. "Who goes where?"

"I'll go after the Ring," Riq said. He felt like he had to be the one to do it, to prove to himself that he was still committed to the mission, in spite of the potential cost.

"It will be in the palace with the vizier," Abi said. "I know my way around, so I will go with you."

"That means Dak and I will get into position so that we'll be able to reach Hulagu," Sera said. "Right. We can totally do this."

Riq grasped the handle on the door. "Ready?"

Everyone nodded at him.

He opened the door and peered outside. There wasn't anyone around. "Coast is clear," he said. "Good luck, everyone."

He opened the door wider and stepped out into the sunlight, the sounds of the Mongol assault much louder now than they had been in their cell. The crash and boom of the artillery echoed across the city. So did the battle shrieks of their warriors.

Riq and Abi turned toward the palace, while Dak and Sera turned the other direction to head into the city. Riq glanced back at them as they set off, heading toward the danger and destruction.

Just outside the palace, Abi stopped. "I do not know what we will face inside. The caliph may still deny the danger, or he may have surrounded himself with his guards."

"There's only one way to find out," Riq said.

Together, they entered the garden they had seen on their first trip to the palace. The beauty and tranquility of the place felt really weird now when Riq thought about the destruction taking place not too far away. It was like the caliph lived in his own little bubble. He could look at his flowers and pretend that everything was okay.

After that, they passed into the menagerie. But something wasn't quite right. Many of the animals were gone. Or at least, not in their cages. And some of the cages were open.

"It looks as though the animal keepers have fled," Abi whispered.

"So where are the animals?" Riq asked.

"Probably wherever they would feel safer than in a cage." Abi looked around them. At the trees. At the bushes. The tall grass.

Riq imagined eyes peering at him from all directions,

and felt a tingling sensation crawl up his neck. He shook his head. He had to be imagining it. And yet . . .

They proceeded slowly, eyes on the vegetation. There had been tigers in here. Lions. As they reached the far side of the menagerie, they heard a blowing sound ahead of them. Something shook the bushes. Riq and Abi stopped in the path, and both held perfectly still as a black bear lumbered into view.

It looked at them, lifting its nose into the air, nostrils flaring. Then its ears went back flat against its head, and the blowing sound it made got louder. Its teeth clacked together as it swung its head low, back and forth.

"What do we do?" Riq whispered without taking his eyes off it.

"I don't know," Abi said. "It is blocking our exit."

Riq let his gaze leave the bear a moment to look for another way out. He noticed a second-story balcony running the length of one of the menagerie's walls. If they could somehow get up there, they could escape. Riq looked closer, and noticed a tree growing up against the wall that appeared to come within reach of the balcony.

"Abi," he whispered. "What if we climb that tree?"

Abi's eyes widened. "I have never in my life climbed a tree."

"There's a first time for everything," Riq said. "I think I remember somewhere that you're not supposed to turn your back on a bear."

"Rather like the caliph," Abi said, managing a smile.

"Right. So let's back away from the caliph's bear toward that tree."

"Lead the way," Abi said.

Riq slid one foot backward, then the other, inching away from the bear. Abi followed. The bear watched them without moving, still blowing and clacking. As the distance grew between the animal and them, Riq took larger and larger steps, gaining confidence. But that feeling was short-lived as the bear decided to lope toward them a few paces.

"Stay calm," Abi said. "It is not charging us."

"Don't make eye contact." That was something else Riq remembered from somewhere. Probably a nature show he'd watched with his grandma. "They perceive it as a challenge."

"Also like the caliph," Abi said, but without the smile.

A few steps later, Riq reached the tree. He didn't know what kind it was, but it had branches low enough to reach, and that was all that mattered.

"Abi," he said. "You go up first."

"No," he said. "You go. I may need you to pull me up."

Riq hesitated, but decided that if this was Abi's first time climbing a tree, it would be easier to pull him than push him. He reached up to the nearest branch, still facing the bear as fully as he could. The bark felt smooth in his hands.

"Here I go." In one smooth motion, Riq turned, kicked against the trunk, and pulled himself up onto the branch.

He swung one of his legs over it and sat upright, feet dangling to either side. Then he lifted his knees, one at a time, and got his feet under him. He braced himself against the trunk. "Okay, Abi. I can help you now."

Abi darted a look up at him. Then the Hystorian stretched his hands toward the branch, only barely managing to reach it. Through the leaves, Riq watched the bear getting closer, ears still back, head still swinging.

"Use the trunk like I did," Riq said.

Abi adjusted his grip on the branch, and then kicked at the trunk, but his shoes just scraped it, and he ended up doing a little bicycle pedal in the air, hanging from the branch. The bear circled around the tree, watching him.

"Try again," Riq said. "Kick higher."

Abi made another leap, and this time it worked. He managed to get his chest up onto the branch, his elbows hanging over it, the rest of him dangling. His face was red, his cheeks puffing with his heavy breathing.

Riq bent down and grabbed his robes. "Don't let go. Try to lift your leg up so I can grab it."

Abi grunted and swung his leg. Riq bent down and snatched for it, but couldn't reach it.

"Higher," he said. The bear came closer. "Higher, Abi."

The Hystorian let out a low rumble that turned to a growl, then a roar as he closed his eyes and heaved his leg up. Riq managed to snag Abi's pants, and after that it was easy enough to pull his leg up over the branch and help him stand up.

They both looked down at the bear. It circled around the base of the tree, sniffing, and then it stood up on its hind legs, front claws raking the trunk.

"Oh," Riq said with a sinking feeling. "That's right. Bears climb trees."

The Grand Vizier

RIQ PERCHED on the branch, which was now bouncing and creaking under his and Abi's combined weight. The black bear below them had dug its claws into the bark of the tree, and had started climbing after them.

"You are right," Abi said. "They *do* climb trees."

"Let's go!" Riq reached for the next branch and climbed higher.

It was easier now, because they could use the other branches like steps on a ladder. Abi was able to keep up on his own, but he was already out of breath. The bear, on the other hand, did not seem to be slowing down at all.

Riq made it to the branch closest to the balcony's wooden railing. He reached out with one of his hands while holding on to the tree with the other, and grabbed it. Then he pushed off of the tree and pulled himself across the space between them, his toes landing right on the ledge. After that, it was easy to climb over the railing. He just didn't know if it would be easy for Abi.

He turned back to the Hystorian and reached out his hand. "Hurry! The bear is—"

"Thank you." Abi's knuckles were white as he inched along the branch toward Riq. "But I am trying very hard not to think about what the bear is doing or wants to do."

"Right," Riq said. "Sorry." But the bear was getting really close. And those claws looked long and mean.

"All right," Abi said. "I think I am ready."

"I'm here." Riq reached out farther.

Abi stretched and grasped Riq's hand like they were about to arm wrestle. It was a bit sweaty, and Riq hoped he could hold on.

"On your count," Riq said.

The bear was only one branch below Abi now.

Abi nodded and exhaled. "All right. On three. One. Two. THREE!"

Abi jumped toward the balcony. Riq yanked on his arm, and the Hystorian crossed the gap, landing on the ledge. But a second later, his toes slipped.

"Abi!" Riq still held on to him, and it felt like something tore in his shoulder as the Hystorian's weight almost pulled him over the railing. Riq cried out as searing pain shot up and down his arm. But he refused to let go. He would not let go.

"Come on." Riq spoke through gritted teeth. "You gotta help me here."

The Hystorian dangled as the bear reached the tree branch where they had just been. It beat the branch with its paw, sending little chips of wood flying. Could it make the jump?

Riq's grip began to fail. "Abi, come on, man."

"I . . . am trying," the Hystorian said. "I just . . . need to . . . grab the railing."

Riq braced himself for the pain, propped one foot against the railing, and pushed backward, lifting Abi a little bit higher. The pain in his shoulder got so bad he worried he might black out.

"There!" Abi got his other hand on to the railing. With Riq still pulling, he heaved himself over the railing, bent at the waist. From there, he simply tumbled onto the balcony, and Riq went down with him. He fell onto his back, and lay there for a moment. The pain had eased up in his shoulder a bit, but it flared again as soon as he tried to move it.

"The bear does not seem inclined to make the jump," Abi said.

Riq looked up, grimacing. The Hystorian was right. The bear had stayed where it was, just watching them. They'd escaped. He dropped his head back down.

"You are injured," Abi said.

"My shoulder," Riq said.

"May I?" Abi knelt down beside him and gently felt Riq's entire side, his arm, and then his shoulder.

Riq winced.

"It is dislocated," Abi said. "But I can put it back."

"Do it," Riq said.

"It will hurt," Abi said. "But then it will feel better."

Riq lifted up his good arm and bit down hard on the sleeve of his coat. He closed his eyes, and he nodded.

Abi took Riq's arm in a very firm grip, and then knelt on Riq's shoulder. The pain burst white-hot, blinding. Riq felt like his whole side was twisting up in a spasm, then he felt a popping. And then the pain was gone. Abi released him.

"There," he said.

"Th—" Riq's voice came out a croak. "Thank you."

"No," Abi said. "Thank you. You didn't let me go."

Riq sat up, blinking, testing his shoulder. It was still incredibly tender, but he no longer felt the same stabbing pain. He staggered to his feet.

"Right," he said. "Now, let's go find the vizier."

Abi led them from room to room, each time scouting a bit ahead for any sign of the palace guards. So far, they hadn't seen anyone else. The place seemed deserted.

"I don't get it," Riq said. "Where is everybody?"

"I don't know," Abi said. "But the vizier will be with the caliph. The SQ is too close to victory to let him out of their sight now. They won't risk anything going wrong."

"So where is the caliph?" Riq asked.

Abi smiled, as if a realization had dawned on him. "Like the bear, he will go where he feels safe. Follow me."

The Hystorian moved forward without any hesitation, and Riq fell in step with him. They took a few turns, and ended up in a familiar place, just a room away from the garden where they had met the caliph the first time.

"Are you serious?" Riq said. "He's here? When the Mongols are about to take the city?"

Abi nodded. "He'll have everyone in there with him. His family. His guards. But like the bear, he feels threatened and may charge."

"So how do we get to the vizier?"

Abi's wide smile returned. "We get the vizier to come to us. Just follow my lead."

He lifted his head high and strode ahead. Riq did the same, and they entered the garden.

It looked just as it had days earlier, except more armed guards blocked their way. Lots more. They formed a wall around the caliph's tent in the middle of the garden. As Riq stood there, a frightened-looking servant dashed up and spritzed him with that same rose water from before. Riq couldn't believe it. This whole thing seemed insane.

"What is the meaning of—" The vizier trundled toward them from inside the ring of guards, but stopped short when he saw them. "How did—?"

"The SQ is not the only organization with spies and allies," Abi said. "Our forces are here, too. Some, even in this very garden."

The vizier's mouth opened, and he glanced over both shoulders.

"I just wanted to give you fair warning," Abi said. "We're coming for you."

Abi turned around and walked away. Riq watched the vizier's reaction turn from fear to anger. The SQ agent actually began to tremble.

"Come!" Abi called to Riq, and Riq followed after the Hystorian. "Walk calmly," Abi whispered. "But be ready to run. In a moment, the vizier will recover from the surprise."

A moment later, they heard the vizier shout behind them, "SEIZE THOSE TWO!"

"Now we run," Abi said.

They sprinted forward, racing through the palace. Riq got completely disoriented, but Abi seemed to know exactly where he was going, so Riq just stuck closely to him. A backward glance revealed four guards and the vizier charging after them.

"Do you have a plan?" Riq asked, panting hard.

"I am making one," Abi said. "For now, keep running."

Riq decided he better start thinking about a plan of his own. There was no way they could handle four guards and the vizier, just the two of them.

They rounded a corner and skidded to a halt. It was a dead end. Abi frowned at the wall as if it were simply a fact he disagreed with. "This should not be here."

"It's here," Riq said. "Let's go." They ran back, retracing

their footsteps, and entered into a long, narrow room, coming face-to-face with the vizier and his guards.

"If you have so many behind you"—the vizier wheezed as he spoke—"then why do you run?" He turned to the guards. "Take them."

But just then, something growled behind the guards, low and menacing. They all turned to look at the same time, and between them, Riq saw a tiger. It was huge. Twice as big as the bear had been. Its whole face lifted in a snarl, exposing its fangs, and it held its body low to the ground, stalking forward, ready to pounce.

"RUN!" one of the guards shouted, and the four of them flew right past Riq and Abi, almost knocking them down.

The vizier stood paralyzed. The tiger roared, sounding as loud to Riq as an entire Mongol army.

"We should run, too," Abi said, and Riq agreed.

They shot down a different hallway than the guards had gone, and heard the vizier behind them. "Wait for me!"

A few yards ahead, they came to a staircase. Riq took it four steps at a time, and they came up onto another balcony. This one was narrow, with no railing, and overlooked a small courtyard. The frightened screams of the vizier and the roaring of the tiger echoed behind them. Riq looked around, and noticed a tapestry hanging from the wall. It gave him an idea, and he ripped it down.

"Take the other end!" he said to Abi.

Together, they stretched it across the door. Riq heard footsteps on the stairs.

"When they hit it, you let go," Riq said.

Abi shifted on his feet and nodded.

Riq was pretty sure this was going to hurt his shoulder like nothing else.

The vizier's footsteps and screaming reached the top of the staircase, and the tapestry exploded outward. Abi let go of his end, and the vizier careened forward, arms pinwheeling, to the very edge of the balcony. The tiger leapt out of the stairwell right behind him, seemed to notice the ledge, and slipped on its feet. But the momentum of its weight carried it along the floor. It scrambled, paws and claws splayed, but went over the side with a roar.

The vizier, still teetering, grabbed the tapestry as he fell, and Riq cried out at the pain in his shoulder. But it wasn't as bad as before. It wasn't dislocated.

The vizier clung to the tapestry as the beast, which had apparently landed just fine, paced around the court-yard below.

"I'm telling you right now!" Riq shouted down to the vizier. "I've been lifting Abi all day, and I can't hold you forever!"

"Please!" the vizier shouted. "Don't drop me!"

"Where is the device you took from us?" Riq asked.

"I have it! It is here!"

"Hand it up!" Riq said.

"Are you mad?" The vizier's voice completely broke. "I would have to let go!"

"Only with one hand!" Riq said.

The vizier let out a pathetic sob. "I can't."

The muscles in Riq's arms started to quiver. He had been telling the truth: He couldn't hold on much longer. But he wasn't really planning to feed the guy to the tiger either. He just hoped the vizier would give in before Riq had to pull him up.

The tiger roared again below them, eyeing the vizier's dangling feet. The animal actually made a leap for him, but missed, and the vizier screamed.

"He might jump higher next time!" Riq shouted.

"All right!" the vizier shrieked. He let go of the tapestry with one hand, hanging by the other, reached into his robes, and pulled out the Ring. Riq nodded to Abi, and the Hystorian came forward, reached down, and took the Ring from the vizier's hand. As soon as the vizier had let go of the device, he clamped both hands back on the tapestry.

"Thank you!" Riq said. He looked at Abi. "Help me lift him up."

Together, they hauled the tapestry onto the balcony, along with the very frightened vizier. The man kissed the ground and then stood up. Riq watched him, wary.

"It would seem the Hystorians have some scruples," the vizier said. "I, on the other hand, do not."

He lunged for the Ring, still in Abi's hands, and the

two of them fought over it along the narrow balcony. Riq panicked. Damaging the SQuare was one thing, but they could *not* break the Ring. He jumped into the tug-of-war, and worked on loosening the vizier's hands.

The man wrenched and pulled, and Riq pried the vizier's fingers away one at a time, until the last came free. When that happened, the vizier stumbled backward, and this time, there wasn't a tapestry to hold on to. Riq watched, helpless, as the man fell wide-eyed over the ledge. Screams and roaring followed, but Riq tried not to listen, and he definitely didn't want to look.

He and Abi left the balcony and descended the staircase. Neither of them spoke as they made their way back through the palace, toward the House of Wisdom.

He had completed his part of the mission, and gotten the Infinity Ring back. He only hoped Sera and Dak were okay. The Break now rested on them.

Farid

SERA HAD no idea how they were supposed to do this. It wasn't hard to know where they needed to go. The sounds of the battle waging at the wall gave them the direction. But once the Mongols breached the city, how would Dak and Sera get close to Hulagu? Especially with Guo Kan there. They needed some kind of disguise.

"Hulagu had epilepsy," Dak said.

"Hmm." Sometimes, Sera found it hard to fake interest in Dak's random trivia. "I don't really see how that fact is particularly useful right now."

"It might be," Dak said. "One of my facts just got us out of that prison cell."

Sera didn't have the energy to argue with him. "Fine, Dak. Fine."

They walked down empty streets that had been completely choked with people and camels only a few days before. It seemed like everyone had either fled the city or were hiding inside their houses.

"What's been bothering you?" Dak asked.

"What do you mean?" Sera asked.

"Come on, dude. You know what I mean."

They'd been friends forever. Of course Dak would know that something was wrong. A heaviness fell over Sera and she took a deep breath. "Okay."

"Okay, what?"

"Okay, I'll tell you." She stopped in the street and turned to face him. "But this is a secret between you and me, understand?"

"What level of security clearance?" He chuckled. "Remember? Like when we used to —"

"I'm serious, Dak."

He tipped his head downward, looking at the ground. "Sorry. Okay." Then he looked back up, his smile gone. "What is it?"

Sera paused another moment to make sure he wasn't about to crack another joke. "I saw the Cataclysm during a warp."

Dak's eyebrows lifted. "What do you mean? Like, you *saw* it, saw it?"

"Yes, it was real." Sera closed her eyes, trying to push away the images rising up in her memory. "I was there."

"How?"

"It was when I warped away with Ilsa. I hadn't meant to, but I went to the future."

"Wow." Dak shook his head. "I don't know what to say.

That's . . . big. Why didn't you say anything until now?"

"Because it was bad. Really, really bad. We may have fixed a bunch of Breaks, but the world is still going to be destroyed. As much as we've managed to get right, it isn't nearly enough. I guess I just didn't want to burden you guys with that."

Dak nodded, frowning a little. "But there's something else, isn't there?"

Sera ran her fingers through her hair. "Yes. There's something else." She felt her throat tightening just thinking about what she was going to say. Saying it made it real. But she wasn't going to cry. No tears. "I saw my parents."

"Your . . . they're alive?"

"Yes," Sera said. *No tears.* "No. They died in the Cataclysm."

"I don't understand."

"I think something we did saved them, one of the Breaks we fixed. But it's not enough. If I want to *really* save them, I have to stop the Cataclysm."

"You mean *we* have to stop the Cataclysm," Dak said. "We're in this together."

Sera inhaled sharply. "I know."

Dak smiled at her, and for a moment it felt like they were back home in their tree. Back before they knew anything about Hystorians or Breaks. Back before all of this started.

"Hey!" he said. "I just thought of something. Your parents might be there in the present. Right now. That means you might get to see them when we go back to get a new SQuare!"

That did it. Sera couldn't stop the tears after that. She cried, and Dak apologized, but it wasn't his fault. Sera had already had that same thought many, many times. It made her so happy she almost couldn't stand it. It was too much. Dak put his arms around her and pulled her into a tight hug that lasted a couple of moments, just the right amount of time, before he let her go.

"We're going to save them," he said. "And we're going to save my parents, too. We're going to save the whole world."

Sera cleared her throat and wiped the tears from her cheeks on her sleeve. "Right. That's what we're going to do. So let's do it."

Dak looked around. "I think the Persian Tower is that way." He pointed down the road. "That's where Hulagu will come into the city."

"Then that's where we should go," Sera said.

They set off down the street, the sounds of the battle echoing around them, sounding closer to Sera with every step. They did pass other people occasionally in the street, but the strangers avoided them and hurried by.

A short while later, they came to an intersection towered over by another of the large archways. As they drew closer to it, they saw a man pacing back and forth beneath it, and they soon recognized him. It was Farid, the rug merchant who'd helped them escape the Market Inspector.

When he saw them, he lifted his hands toward them. "Little *pirashki*! Is it you?"

"It's us, Farid," Sera said. "What are you—?"

"Oh, I had almost given up hope! The man and the woman said you would come, but then you didn't come, and I began to doubt my memory of their instructions. I feared I had been waiting in the wrong place!"

"A man and woman?" A chill raced down Dak's back.

"Yes," Farid said. "Two days ago they came to me and gave me ten whole dinar—ten!—and told me to wait here for you. They said you would be coming this way, and I was to give you shelter."

Sera gasped. "Dak, your parents."

"I know," Dak said. "They were here."

"So come, little *pirashki*, come." Farid led them away from the archway. "We will go somewhere safe to wait until this is all over."

But they didn't have time. They couldn't wait until it was over. "Farid," Sera said, "we appreciate—"

"Your concern for us," Dak said, butting in. He leaned in close to Sera and whispered, "We have to trust my parents. Okay?"

Sera thought about it and agreed. Of course they had to trust Dak's parents. So they followed Farid down several streets that twisted and turned, narrowed and widened, until they came to a modest-looking building.

"My home," he said. He unlocked the door and ushered them inside.

The room was dim, but Sera's eyes quickly adjusted.

They were in a kind of entryway, and Farid led them across it to another door, which opened onto a small, square courtyard. Plants grew in large pots in all the corners, and each of the four walls had a doorway. Staircases climbed up the walls to doorways on the second story. For as many rooms as the home had, it seemed to Sera that there should be more people there.

"Do you have a family, Farid?" Sera asked.

He nodded, noticeably calmer since they had gotten off the street. "Yes, I do. But I sent them away from the city the moment I learned the Mongols were coming."

"Why didn't you leave with them?" Dak asked.

"I could not leave my home or my rugs," Farid said. "Besides, I'm sure the city will survive. The caliph knows best, and Baghdad's walls are strong. The Mongols will give up this siege and move on."

"Um," Dak said. "We sure hope so. But it might be smart to prepare for the worst, just in case."

"I am prepared. I have food and water to last me. Are you hungry?"

Actually, Sera was feeling pretty hungry after a few days of eating nothing but the food they'd been given in their prison cell. "Yes, I think we're both hungry."

"What would you like?" Farid asked. "Nothing is cooked, but I have breads, olives, fruit, cheeses—"

"Cheeses?" The excitement in Dak's voice made Sera smile.

"Yes," Farid said. "Come, we will eat, and then you will rest."

Farid's food was delicious, and his hospitality and friendliness put Sera at ease. She was almost able to forget they were basically sitting in the middle of a war zone. Sera didn't know what she and Dak were supposed to be doing there, or how long they should stay, but she decided to wait a little while to see what developed.

Dak had no trouble settling in. Aside from the cheeses, Sera thought being here probably made him feel closer to his parents, because he was where they had wanted him to be.

As dusk arrived, and Farid lit a few oil lamps, Sera decided that she and Dak should at least spend the night. If their purpose in being here wasn't obvious by the next day, they could leave and get back to figuring out how to fix the Break on their own.

She fell asleep easily in the comfortable bed Farid prepared for her and woke up the next day after a deep and restful sleep. She'd even slept through the sounds of the Mongol assault.

"This is the fifth day," Dak said next to her.

That meant in two more days, Hulagu would be there.

"What should we do?" Dak asked.

"I don't know," Sera said. "Last night I thought we should leave today." But lying there in her comfortable bed, and already looking forward to breakfast, Sera had second thoughts. "We can't talk to Hulagu until he's in the city. There's no way we can get to him now."

"So you think we should wait?" Dak asked.

"It seems like that's what your parents wanted us to do."

"I was thinking the same thing."

Sera let her eyes close again. "Then let's wait."

That day and the next came and went. Sera and Dak ate. They slept. Farid told them wonderful stories to try to distract them, and they played chess. But the whole time Sera worried about Riq, and with the distant sounds of the Mongol army, she never felt at ease.

On the morning of the seventh day of the siege, Sera woke up feeling especially anxious. This was the day Hulagu would take the Persian Tower and move into the city. Sera and Dak still had to find a way to get to him. It was time for them to leave.

"Wake up, Dak." She shook him.

His eyes stayed closed. "No."

"Dak, we need to get going."

"Why?"

"We have a Break to fix."

"I think we should stay here until we know what my parents wanted us to do," Dak said.

"But we don't know how long that will take," Sera said. "And besides, your parents aren't thinking about the Breaks. They're thinking about you, and we don't have a lot of time."

"I know, but—"

A pounding on the front door echoed through the whole house, followed by the sound of a man's voice shouting. "Farid! Rug Merchant!"

Sera and Dak got to their feet and walked out of their room into the courtyard. Farid was already at the front door. He looked back, and motioned for them to step aside, out of view.

Farid opened the door. "Ah, Market Inspector, what an unexpected honor to have you at my home."

Market Inspector? But he was SQ! How had he found them here? This could not be happening, Sera thought, not after they had finally escaped the grand vizier.

"Spare me your flattery," the Market Inspector said. "You know why I have come."

Little *Pirashki*

DAK TRIED to control the panic rising up inside him. The Market Inspector was here. He had tracked them down. Or had Farid betrayed them? Dak didn't want to believe that, not when his parents were the ones who had made sure he ended up here.

"I apologize," Farid said. "But I do not know why you have come."

"I've come to confiscate your rugs," the Inspector said.

"Confiscate? My rugs? But why?"

"They are needed by Hulagu Khan." The Inspector's voice sounded just as snobby and annoying as Dak remembered it. "He who will shortly breach the city. There is a palace being prepared for him on the eastern side of town, and for this palace we need rugs. Your rugs."

"I am happy to offer my rugs to Hulagu Khan," Farid said. "Give me some time to prepare them."

"We'll be back in one hour," the Market Inspector said. "Have them ready."

The front door shut, and Farid came back into the courtyard. Dak and Sera stepped out from their hiding place.

"That scoundrel!" Farid punched the palm of his hand. "My rugs! For that warlord?"

"Actually . . ." Sera said.

Dak turned to look at her. She had that look in her eyes, the one she got when she was about to solve a great big math problem.

"Do you need a couple of carpet inspectors?" she asked. "One more time?"

Dak saw where she was going. And it was *perfect*.

Before the Market Inspector returned, Farid helped them get rolled up in two carpets and loaded onto a cart with the rest of the rugs going to Hulagu Khan's new palace. He hitched a donkey up to the cart, and it just so happened that its rear end sat right in front of Dak's carpet. Like, inches away from his face, and of course, he couldn't move his face to escape it. What was it with beasts of burden and this Break?

"Are you sure about this, little *pirashki*?" Farid asked. He sounded really nervous to Dak.

"We're sure, Farid," Dak said. Maybe he could wiggle his hand up to plug his nose if he needed to. . . .

"Thank you for everything, Farid," Sera said. "I hope the ten dinar is enough."

"Ten dinar?" Farid laughed. "That's a small fortune! But I would have helped you children for nothing. You are good, and the Market Inspector is bad, and I wish I knew why you were doing this."

"We told you," Sera said. "And it's a secret no one else can know."

"Ah, your story about the djinn and the ring that can move through time?"

"Yes," Dak said. His story had sounded better when he told it the second time, to Farid. They had been trying to find a way to explain their mission.

"Well, do not be offended," Farid said, "but a children's story like that does little to reassure me."

"Trust us," Sera said. "We—"

"Shh," Farid said. "The Market Inspector comes."

They fell silent, and a few moments later, the Market Inspector's voice came from right beside the cart.

"Well done, Rug Merchant," he said. "You have made the right decision."

"Allow me to transport my wares to the great khan's palace?" Farid asked.

"Certainly," the Market Inspector said. "I shall accompany you."

A moment later, the donkey brayed, and the cart lurched forward, tipping and rocking along the road. Dak stayed as motionless and silent as he could. He could almost feel Sera inside her rug next to him. The cart moved slowly, so slowly it began to drive Dak crazy. He didn't like not being able to see outside. He didn't like not knowing what was going on.

But after what felt like forever, the cart rocked to a stop, and the Market Inspector cleared his throat.

"Hulagu Khan appreciates your offering, Rug Merchant," he said. "For it, you shall be spared. You may stay here following the siege, where you will be safe from the pillaging to come."

"Th-thank you?" Farid said.

That actually made Dak feel good. By helping them, perhaps Farid had helped himself.

"Leave the rugs here," the Market Inspector said. "I'll have someone attend to them."

Uh-oh. That would not be good.

"Uh — that is, I could take care of that," Farid said. He sounded a little flustered. Was it enough to make the Market Inspector suspicious? "I find pleasure in seeing the places my rugs will be enjoyed, you see."

The Market Inspector was silent. Dak waited.

"Very well," the Market Inspector said. "That will save me the trouble. They are intended for Hulagu Khan's reception hall."

"Excellent!" Farid clapped his hands. "The more people to see my rugs!"

"Yes, indeed." The Market Inspector sounded like he had already lost interest in the rugs. "Carry on. I have important work to attend to. But I shall be back to examine them, and if I find any of them to be lacking in quality, I shall be very displeased. I maintain a very high standard in the markets of Baghdad and for the khan."

"Yes, *muḥtasib*," Farid said.

There was silence for a long time. And then Dak heard Farid sigh. "I'm taking you both straight into the lion's den," he said. "I feel like I should ask you to forgive me."

Over the next little while, Farid loaded the rugs, one by one, into Hulagu's new palace. That meant there were several periods where he was gone, and Dak and Sera were alone in the cart, hoping no one stopped to examine the rugs. They didn't dare whisper to each other, even though they wanted to.

Eventually, Farid came back and said, "All right, up we go." Dak felt him hoist Sera away from him, out of the cart with a grunt. "My, what a heavy rug," Farid said then, chuckling.

Dak smiled. Then he was alone. Really alone.

He tried to ignore the donkey rear taking up his vision, and pictured instead where they might be. Their surroundings. Maybe they were in the street. Maybe they were in a courtyard. He tried to imagine what was going on. Where his parents might be. Where they had gone after they'd given the dinars to Farid. Were they already ahead of them at the next Break? Dak started wondering what that might be, too. Where would they go, and what would they see? His thoughts felt like a runaway train sometimes. Just completely unstoppable.

He heard footsteps returning, and braced himself to be lifted in the air.

"*Hmph,*" a voice said. "One rug left."

Oh, no! No, this could not be happening! Dak sucked in a breath. It was the Market Inspector!

"You there! Guard!" the Market Inspector shouted. "Come move this rug inside so we can clear this cart from the courtyard. I don't want it here when Hulagu Khan arrives."

Where was Farid? Dak began to really panic now.

"Yes, *muḥtasib,*" another man said. His footsteps came closer.

Okay, stay calm. Dak would just go limp. Become one with the rug. Maybe the guy wouldn't notice. Maybe he'd just carry him right on inside. Dak relaxed every muscle in his body, down to the tips of his fingers.

He felt hands reach around him, and then a squeezing as the hands lifted him from the cart.

"*Omph!*" the guard said. "Heavy rug!"

"Excellent," the Market Inspector said. "A heavy rug is a high-quality rug. Farid really did bring his best. Guo Kan will be most pleased. The happier we keep Hulagu, the stronger our position. Take it inside to the audience hall."

"Yes, *muḥtasib.*"

Dak rolled and the world spun, and then he came to rest high up, probably on the guard's shoulder. As scared as Dak was, and as fast as his heart raced, he kept his body as loose as a noodle, bouncing a little with each of the guard's steps.

Moments later, Dak heard voices up ahead.

"My—my rug!" That was Farid. "You did not have to bring it to me. I would have unloaded it myself."

"The Market Inspector asked me."

"The . . . Market Inspector?"

"Yes, but since you're here, would you mind taking it?"

"YES!" Farid shouted. "I mean, of course."

Dak rolled again, downward, and came to rest at a lower spot. He could tell Farid held him now.

"That's a high-quality rug," the guard said.

"Th-thank you," Farid said.

Dak heard the scuff of the guard's boot as he turned and walked away, the echo of his footsteps receding.

"*Pirashki?*" Farid whispered.

"I'm here," Dak whispered back.

Farid sighed and carried Dak a little ways before setting him down. "We are alone," the rug merchant said, and unrolled Dak from the rug.

As it opened up and spit Dak out, he kept rolling a couple of times, his legs and arms flopping. Then, between the stress and his desperate attempt to relax, all he could do was just lie there. "I don't know if I'll ever be able to move again," he said to himself.

"Well, you'd better."

He looked up at Sera.

"Hulagu will be here soon."

Dak struggled to his feet, and for the next little while, they helped Farid lay out the rugs, covering the floor of the audience hall. Dak got a look at his surroundings for the first time. The room was tall, with carved, blue-tiled pillars supporting a vaulted ceiling. High windows let light into the rafters, but left everything below in a soft glow. There were some pieces of wooden furniture along the walls, cabinets and chests. Probably meant to hold the tributes and gifts sure to come Hulagu's way. At one end of the room stood a raised platform, with an ornate, upholstered seat. Hulagu's throne. They were definitely in the right place. And almost at the right time.

After that, and with a lot of reassurance, they eventually convinced Farid to leave them alone to wait.

"I almost wish I could have seen it," Dak said.

"What?" Sera asked.

"The battle at the Persian Tower," Dak said. "It's an important moment in history."

"A *violent* moment in history," Sera said. "No thank you."

"Bad things happen," Dak said. "*Really* bad things happen. I mean, just think about how many wars have been fought here in Baghdad." He shook his head. "Ancient wars. And modern wars. You'd think we could learn something from that and not keep making the same mistakes."

"I know bad things happen," Sera whispered. "But I've

seen enough wars now to know *exactly* what they're like, and I don't want to keep seeing them over and over."

"Maybe you're right," Dak said.

Sera pointed over in a corner. "There's an empty cabinet over there. I think we can hide inside it until the right time."

Dak nodded. "Sounds like a plan."

Hulagu Khan

SERA AND Dak hunkered close together inside the cabinet, waiting. It was musty smelling, and old. They knew it was only a matter of time now until Hulagu entered the city and took possession of his temporary palace. Only a matter of time until Sera and Dak had to step out and convince him, somehow, to spare the House of Wisdom.

"Listen to that," Dak said. "The siege has ended."

Sera cocked her ear. He was right. The sounds of battle had gone, and the city was quiet.

"Won't be long now," Dak said. "Hulagu . . ." He shook his head. "Never mind."

"What?" Sera asked.

"Nothing." He looked away. "I was just going to annoy you with another historical fact."

Sera felt a little stab of guilt over the way she'd been treating Dak. Sure, his historical babble annoyed her at times, but it was also something she liked about him, because it was part of what made Dak . . . Dak.

"I'm sorry for the way I've been treating you," she said.

He looked up.

"Riq and I have been kind of ganging up on you. Normally, I've always defended you, but I haven't been a very good best friend lately."

"That's okay," Dak said. "You had the whole seeing your parents and the Cataclysm thing to deal with. It's fine. We're good."

"Are you sure?"

"Of course," Dak said. "And I mean, I know I can be really annoying. I just can't stop it."

"You really like history," Sera said. "And that's okay. That's you."

A few minutes of silence passed. Then Sera asked, "So, what was the fact you were going to tell me?"

"Well" — Dak grinned a little — "it was that —"

But noises outside the cabinet cut him off. The *clomp* of many, many boots, and the din of many voices. It sounded like a wave rushing into the room. It settled all around them, and Sera opened the cabinet just a crack to look out. The room had filled with Mongols, and some people from Baghdad, too. They milled around, talking, waiting. Then, a short while later, they all fell silent at the same moment, and Sera knew that meant Hulagu had entered the room.

Everyone dropped to the ground in a bow, and Sera saw him stride forward with wide, bow-legged steps. He wore flashing, gilded armor, with a jeweled helmet on his head, and a jeweled sword at his waist. Behind him came a train of attendants, including Tusi.

Hulagu climbed to his throne and sat down. The entire room stayed bowed as his imperious gaze swept across them. "You may rise," he said at last.

What followed appeared to be some kind of ritual, where generals and warriors came forward, and Hulagu praised them for doing something extraordinary on the battlefield. Then they exchanged gifts, and the gifts were almost always clothing of some kind. The fancier the item, the higher the honor, with some hats and coats appearing to be made entirely of gold thread and gem-stones. So Hulagu gave gifts to his people, and the people gave gifts to Hulagu.

"What's going on out there?" Dak asked. He couldn't see like she could.

She tried to describe what she was seeing, and Dak nodded along, but she could tell he was frustrated.

"Are you okay?" she asked.

"I just want to know what's going on," he said.

Sera smiled. That was very true of Dak. Everywhere they went, he was always trying to figure things out, and usually he did that by relating whatever was going on back to history in some way.

"Okay," she whispered, willing to try harder for him. "Now there's a guy giving Hulagu a long coat with a peacock embroidered on it. Lots of silver thread."

Dak sat back, listening, and this went on for a long time. So long, Sera actually started to get bored, and she yawned.

"This could go on forever," she said. "What should we do?"

"Keep waiting?"

Sera didn't want to keep waiting. Everything depended on them getting this right. They'd planned to try to find a time when Hulagu would be alone, but that didn't seem to be happening anytime soon. Maybe not at all.

"I think we should do it now," she said.

"Here?" Dak straightened. "In front of everybody?"

"Yes," Sera said.

Dak rubbed his head with both hands. "Okay. Okay, let's do it."

Sera opened the cabinet door, and they slipped out of it. Everyone in the room was facing the khan, so nobody noticed them at first. They managed to glide along the wall, getting closer and closer to the throne.

But then Sera made eye contact with a warrior, and he nudged the guy next to him, and that guy turned to stare. Then he tapped the guy in front of him, and that man shouted.

"You! What are you doing here?"

The attention of the entire room swiveled toward them, and everyone fell silent. Sera thought maybe this was a bad idea, after all. Her stomach sank. Was this how

Dak felt when one of his ideas didn't pan out the way he'd hoped?

"What is the meaning of this?" Another man marched toward them with a very hard and menacing gait. "Who let these children in?"

"I don't know, General Guo Kan," the warrior said, bowing. "I just saw them creeping toward the great khan."

So this was the Time Warden. Guo Kan. When he drew near, he recognized Dak immediately. "So, you've come back," he said. "I appreciate prisoners who return to their cells. I see you now have the girl with you but are missing the African. Where is he?"

"Defeating the vizier as we speak," Dak said.

"I doubt that," Guo Kan said. "But you, you have disrupted an important ceremony." His voice fell to a deep growl. "So I will deal with you personally."

"Bring them here!"

Sera, along with everyone in the room, turned toward the throne. Hulagu stood, staring at them. Waiting.

Guo Kan clearly felt torn. He obviously didn't want Sera and Dak anywhere near the khan, but Sera also figured he couldn't disobey Hulagu's order either.

"Yes, my lord," the general said. He grabbed Sera and Dak by the arms, one in each hand, and dragged them forward until they stood before the throne.

Sera dropped to her knees, bowing, and Dak did the same.

"What are you doing here?" Hulagu asked.

"They are spies, great khan," Guo Kan said. "Sent to assassinate you."

"Children?" Hulagu said. "Assassins?"

"I think not," came a calm voice from the side of the throne.

Sera looked up as Tusi stepped forward, his hands clasped behind his back. She was shocked. Was he actually sticking his neck out to help them?

Tusi cleared his throat. "My reading of the stars foretold an unexpected visit to your court, great khan. What are these children if not unexpected? I believe they may be a portent, possibly sent to you for a reason known only to your gods. How you deal with them may have lasting importance to your reign."

Hulagu looked at Tusi. "I see."

Tusi *was* helping them! He made eye contact with Sera, his expression unreadable. Angry? Sad? Frightened? He spoke again. "I would like to consult the stars again, great khan. I advise you take no action until I have had the opportunity to study the matter."

Hulagu returned to his throne. "Very well. Your reading of the heavens has guided me true until this point. I shall put my trust in you again, Tusi."

Tusi bowed. "I am honored, great khan. May I interview these children in private?"

Guo Kan's face burned red. "Great khan, I would urge—"

"Yes," Hulagu said. "You may interview them in private."

Tusi looked at the general, who released Sera and Dak as roughly as he had grabbed them.

"With your leave, great khan," Tusi said, "I will take them now."

"Yes, yes," Hulagu said. "Go."

Tusi bowed. He motioned for Sera and Dak to bow, which they did, and then they left the audience hall through a little side door. Tusi led them into an adjacent room, and after he had shut the door, he spun on them with rage that seemed barely controlled.

"Do you know what you have done?" he asked.

Sera felt herself withering, but recovered quickly. They had done nothing wrong. In fact, they were doing the exact right thing. It was Tusi who had made the wrong choices.

"We're doing what we have to," Sera said, "to save the House of Wisdom."

Tusi groaned. "What madness is this? Forget the House of Wisdom! There is nothing you can do! But now you've come here and put your lives in danger, and I foolishly stepped out to defend you, putting my life in danger as well!"

"We didn't mean to put your life in danger," Sera said.

"Yeah," Dak said. "What's your problem? We didn't ask for your help."

"The general would have made swift work of you if I had not intervened, believe me. He was not pleased with your previous escape."

Dak smirked. "No?"

"No. He executed the warriors who failed to guard you."

"Oh." Dak's smile crumbled.

"But that is not your fault," Tusi said. "You simply have no idea the nature of the men you deal with. Guo Kan is merciless. And Hulagu does not see the world the way you do. You cannot reason with him."

"But you can!" Sera said. "You could do something!"

Tusi made a fist and pressed it against his forehead. "I cannot. It is not my responsibility."

"You're only thinking of yourself," Sera said. "What about your responsibility to science? To knowledge? Those matter to the entire world! Don't you care about that?"

Tusi brought his hand down. "Of course I do." His voice softened. "Since you came to me at the war camp, I have not had a single restful night. My doubts keep me awake. I have spent many hours wondering how I could convince the khan to keep his men out of the libraries, to spare them. But there is nothing I can say that will convince him."

"I can think of something," Dak said.

Sera turned toward him. So did Tusi.

"Hulagu obviously puts a lot of trust in the stars, right? So what do you need to study the stars?"

"Celestial globes," Tusi said. "Charts, tables."

"Right," Dak said. "But what you *really* need is an

observatory. And what does an observatory need?"

Sera saw where Dak was going. And it was brilliant.

Tusi saw it, too. Sera could tell because a smile broke unevenly across his face. "A library," he whispered.

"Right," Dak said. "You just need some books. And I happen to know a place where you can find *lots* of them."

A Dangerous Proposal

Dak was on a roll. First he'd busted them all out of that prison, and now he'd managed to convince Tusi to help them, and even given him the way to do it. Now Dak and Sera just had to sit back and let Tusi do his thing and convince Hulagu to build him an observatory, stocked with books from Baghdad.

"We'll wait until the morning to approach the throne," Tusi said. "I will . . . consult the stars. But I already have a fairly good idea of what they will tell me."

"I bet that's usually the way you work," Dak said.

Tusi shrugged. "I am far more interested in predicting the motion of the stars than predicting events from those motions. The former is science, while the latter is nothing more than seeing what we want to see. Now you should both get some rest."

Dak had to admit he was pretty tired. So he and Sera nestled down on some cushions Tusi had a servant bring into the room. These Baghdad beds were growing on him. Who needed a mattress?

Dak closed his eyes, and before long, he nodded off.

Shouting startled him awake. He jumped up, only to feel someone grab him from behind in a bear hug, pinning his arms at his sides.

"Let me go!" he roared, squirming, but it was no use. He was trapped.

Dak looked to his side, and saw that another man had Sera. General Guo Kan stood nearby.

Tusi shook his fist at him. "You dare disobey the great khan!"

"I've had enough of your meddling, Tusi," Guo Kan said. "You may have Hulagu deceived by your superstitious pandering, but you and I both know you're a far more intelligent man than that. But you're also a survivor, and I actually respect that."

"Your respect means nothing to me," Tusi said. "And you know something of superstition yourself, don't you, Divine Man?" Dak heard sarcasm all over the way Tusi said the name.

"We both play our parts," Guo Kan said. "Go back to playing yours, as you do so well, and you might manage to survive once more. Leave the children to me."

"I can't do that," Tusi said. "They're children."

"And they are more dangerous than you realize." Guo Kan fixed Dak with that same cold stare. "You were right in that, Tusi, even though you don't understand why."

"You will release them now," Tusi said. "And we will take this matter up before the khan."

"Why?" Guo Kan said. "So you can feed him one of your celestial readings?"

Dak tried once more to break free, but the Mongol who had him was strong. It didn't even work to kick or stomp the guy's feet. How was it that just hours ago, they'd seemed so close to victory, but now they perched at the edge of losing it all?

Dak looked at Sera. She was crying, and he knew why. Losing it all meant something more to her. He had to do something. For her.

Guo Kan was trying to get away with something without Hulagu's knowledge. So Dak had to get the khan's attention. He only hoped the warlord was close by.

Dak sucked in a deep breath. "GREAT HULAGU KHAN!" His shout echoed in the small room, as loud as he could make it. "GREAT HULAGU KHAN!"

"Silence him!" Guo Kan hissed.

The guard holding Dak tried to cover his mouth, but Dak just bit his hand and got one more shout off.

"GREAT HULAGU KHAN!"

And then Sera took up the cry, too, screaming in her higher-pitched voice. "HULAGU! GREAT HULAGU KHAN!"

Guo Kan's face twisted up with rage, and he pulled

his sword free of its scabbard. Dak gulped. He didn't think the general would actually kill them right here. But then again, he might.

Tusi took a step backward and laughed out loud. Then he, too, shouted. "MY KHAN! YOUR PEOPLE NEED YOU, GREAT KHAN!"

Guo Kan spun on him. "Now you've gone too far!" He raised his sword.

"NO!" Sera cried.

Tusi lifted his head high. "I see now I have not gone far enough."

"So be it." Guo Kan brought the blade down.

"HALT!"

The walls seemed to reverberate with the force of the command. Hulagu stood in the doorway. Dak's eyes leapt from the warlord back to Tusi and Guo Kan. The general's sword hung poised in the air, mid-strike, inches from Tusi's neck.

"Sheathe that sword," Hulagu said.

Guo Kan lowered his blade and drove it hard into its scabbard.

"What goes on here?" Hulagu asked.

"Tusi and these children conspire against you, great khan," the general said. "I came to stop them."

"That is not true," Tusi said. "Great khan, it is your general who has betrayed your trust. He intended harm to these children, even though you had placed them under your protection."

"Only as I awaited your reading," Hulagu said.

Tusi bowed his head. "Yes, of course."

"Have you completed your reading of the stars?" Hulagu asked.

"I have," Tusi said. "They tell me—"

"Do not trust him, great khan!" the general said. "He means to bend your will to his."

"That is not true!" Tusi shouted.

"Silence!" Hulagu held up both hands. Then he turned to Dak and Sera. "Perhaps it is time I allow these unexpected visitors to speak to me themselves." He looked up at the guy holding Dak. "Release them."

The warrior let Dak out of his grip. The Mongol standing next to Dak released Sera at the same time.

"Thank you, great khan," Dak said.

"I have little patience, boy," Hulagu said. "Why have you come here? How is it you found your way so close to my throne without my permission?"

"How we came here is a very long story," Sera said. "But why we have come is very, very important, great khan."

"Then tell me." Hulagu folded his arms. "Quickly. My patience comes to an end."

Sera looked at Dak. The moment had arrived, the very thing they'd decided they needed to do from the beginning. Hulagu had to be convinced. And Dak thought he knew how. It came back to a question Riq had raised on the road to Baghdad.

Why did Dak like history so much?

"Great khan," Dak said, "this world is a pretty uncertain place. Most events are completely unpredictable. Sometimes it's confusing, and it's hard to know what's going on. I don't like not knowing what's going on. I like to understand things. I use history to help me do that. It's written. It's settled. It happened and that's that. It can help me make sense of things in the present."

Hulagu looked a bit confused, but he said, "Go on."

"You look to the stars for that, right? The heavens are fixed up there. They move across the sky in the same paths, night after night, year after year. You look up to help you know what to do. To help you figure things out. Right?"

Hulagu looked at Tusi. "With the aid of learned men, yes."

"Well," Dak said, "we've come from a distant land with a message for you."

"Who sent you?" Hulagu asked.

"Learned men," Sera said.

"And the message?" Hulagu asked.

"You need to build an observatory," Dak said. "A place where your . . . learned men can study the stars. And give you the best advice."

Hulagu turned to Tusi. "Well? What do you make of this?"

"I am in agreement, great khan. I would be a much better adviser to you if I had a place dedicated to observing the heavens. A true observatory."

"And where would this observatory be located?" Hulagu asked.

"A favorable site would need to be found, but I believe the mountains of Maragheh would be ideal."

"I see," Hulagu said.

"I offer myself, great khan," Tusi said. "I will direct this observatory to your greater glory, to your long life, and to the legacy of your empire."

Dak watched Tusi and had to agree with what Guo Kan had said. The man was a survivor. Tusi would probably come out of this just fine. And it looked like Hulagu was coming around to the idea.

"This proposal appeals to me," Hulagu said.

"The construction will be costly," Tusi said. "To offset the expense to you, might I offer an additional thought?"

"You may," Hulagu said.

"Now that Baghdad has fallen," Tusi said, "the fruits of its many libraries belong to you, and are ripe for plucking. And an observatory under your patronage, the greatest the world has known, should also have a library of great renown."

Dak waited. This was the moment. Right here. History was about to be rewritten. Suddenly, that thought struck Dak in a way it never had before, and he felt like he'd been tipped on his side. Everything was off-kilter. He'd finally realized what history meant to him, and now, that was being taken away from him.

History wasn't settled. Not at all. And Dak was unsettling it.

But without history, what else could he rely on?

Hulagu turned to Guo Kan. "What do you have to say?"

Guo Kan quivered with rage. "Your men have fought valiantly for a share of the riches of Baghdad."

"Books?" Hulagu snorted. "My men do not expect books."

Guo Kan's mouth snapped shut.

"Can you see any objection to this observatory?" Hulagu asked the general.

Guo Kan was in a very dangerous spot, Dak could see that. Hulagu looked to have made up his mind. If the general raised no objection, he failed the SQ, and the Break would be fixed. But if he objected, he risked the khan's wrath. Dak waited anxiously to see what the Time Warden would do, and where his true loyalties lay.

"I do not think this is a wise course," Guo Kan said.

Hulagu scowled. "Then you are not in harmony with me. And you raised your sword against my adviser. For this, you will be imprisoned for a time until I decide what judgment best falls upon you." Hulagu then ordered the two warriors to take Guo Kan into custody.

The general didn't look so divine anymore. He'd finally been defeated. He surrendered his sword and went with the warriors without putting up a fight, and without making eye contact with anyone in the room.

After he was gone, Hulagu said, "My general does make one good point. My men are restless. They hunger for destruction."

"I only need a few days," Tusi said.

"Once the caliph has surrendered," Hulagu said, "I can hold my men back for three days. That is all the time you have to pick your fruit."

Buried Treasure

RIQ WAITED at the House of Wisdom with Abi for days, with no word or sign from Dak and Sera. Many, many times he wanted to go after them, but Abi wouldn't allow it. He said Riq had to safeguard the Infinity Ring, and that meant he couldn't take it anywhere near Guo Kan. Riq thought he could just leave it behind at the House of Wisdom, but Abi insisted that was too risky. In the end, Riq reluctantly agreed with that reasoning.

But he was going pretty crazy wondering what was going on, and feeling pretty helpless. He paced a lot. And he knew a big part of his fear was about what would happen once they finished this Break. He spent hours holding the Infinity Ring. Just staring at it. This device had the power to erase him.

On the seventh day of the siege, the sounds of battle ceased, and Riq walked to a secluded room and sat down, the Infinity Ring in his lap. He tried really hard to believe that Sera and Dak were safe. That they would come soon.

"I'm certain they are well."

Riq looked up. Abi had come into the room.

"I know," Riq said.

"But that is not the only thing troubling you, is it?"

"No," Riq said.

"What else?" Abi asked.

It felt easier to think of telling Abi about it than it did Sera and Dak. "I messed with my own timeline. I'm not sure I exist anymore."

"Of course you exist," Abi said. "You affirm that just by asking the question."

"No," Riq said. "I exist here because we're still in a kind of warp. Dak and Sera and I are slipping through time, and we're not affected yet by what we're doing. But the world we left behind is being affected by everything we do. And when I go back there, I don't know what will happen. I could disappear, like I'd never even been there."

Abi was silent. "That is a heavy burden."

Riq had to laugh. "Yeah. Pretty heavy."

"What will you do?"

"I don't know." Riq rolled the Infinity Ring over. "I've thought about just staying in the past somewhere. I almost did that recently." The image of Kisa came into his mind. How happy he'd been with her. The way she'd felt to him like she filled a Remnant.

"What made you change your mind?"

"I have a mission. I have a responsibility. And I want to honor the sacrifices made by others to get us to this point."

"That is very noble," Abi said.

"Thanks."

"What else could you do?" Abi asked.

Riq shook his head. He frowned. "Just go back. See what happens. Or *not* see what happens."

"I don't understand time travel," Abi said. "But let me ask you this. Are you only a product of the past? Or are you something more? Are you not also the decisions you make right now in the present?"

That was a pretty deep question. But it seemed important. "I guess I'm kind of both."

"Exactly," Abi said. "I believe that even if your past is erased, there is still the part of you that is here, right now, being true and noble, worrying about your friends and seeking to honor them. That makes you real to me."

A knot formed in Riq's throat. He swallowed. "Thanks, Abi."

The next morning, Riq was standing in the courtyard of the House of Wisdom when Dak, Sera, and Tusi walked through the front doors. He laughed and ran toward them, and the three time travelers hugged. There was so much to talk about, but no time. Dak and Sera explained that Hulagu had only given them a few days to save the books in the House of Wisdom.

"The caliph will surrender in four days," Dak said. "Hulagu said he would hold his men off for three days after that."

"I'm not certain how you know that about the caliph," Tusi said. "But I believe you. And that means I have a week to save what I can."

Abi stepped forward. "I'll be happy to assist you. I'm very familiar with the most important volumes in the House of Wisdom." He looked at Riq, Sera, and Dak with a smile.

Riq knew what he meant, those most important volumes being those written by Aristotle about the Great Breaks. It seemed they had succeeded. The Time Wardens had been defeated. The Break was fixed.

"We did it," he said.

"Did you?" came a familiar voice.

Riq turned to see the Market Inspector standing at the entrance, with half a dozen guards at his side. Each of them held a burning torch in his hand, and Riq realized with horror what they planned to do. One way or another, the library would be destroyed, if not by the Mongols, then by the SQ themselves.

"How dare you!" Tusi said. "Hulagu Khan has placed this library under his protection!"

The Market Inspector spread his arms. "Is he here to

protect it? Because all I see are a few children and two scholars."

"Perhaps that's all we need," Abi said. "Tusi, Hystorians, come with me."

They all backed away from the guards, and the Market Inspector laughed. "Run. Run away. Meanwhile, we'll torch this place room by room."

His guards scattered in different directions, and soon, flames began to appear in all the doorways around the courtyard. How many books were burning right now? How much knowledge had just been lost in an instant? Riq raged inside, but there wasn't anything he could do.

"Come!" Abi said. "Follow me!"

He led them deep into the House of Wisdom, through doorways and down hallways Riq had never seen. They eventually took a flight of steps downward and came to a room with a lock on the door. It was a very peculiar lock, with several spinning brass dials filled with scrolling Arabic letters.

Abi rotated the dials. "An invention of the Banū Mūsā brothers. You have to know the secret word to unlock it." A moment later, the dials clicked into place, and the door opened. "Go, go."

Riq smiled. *Open sesame.*

Inside, they found a small room with earthen walls, almost a cave, with another door on the opposite side. Several chests sat in the middle of the floor.

"These contain the works of Aristotle," Abi said. "I gathered them together when you Hystorians first arrived, against the day we might need to move them. We must take these now."

"But the House of Wisdom!" Dak said.

"There is nothing we can do," Abi said. "But these books must survive. And there are many other libraries in Baghdad, with hundreds of thousands of books. Tusi and I will save as many as we can before the Mongols begin their destruction. And we will see that they are copied, so that these words may spread to many libraries in many lands."

Riq thought about what Abi was saying, and realized he was right. This was now the only way. Maybe it had been all along. The important thing was that they would now be able to fix the Prime Break, because the works of Aristotle would survive in a new library. It was like that riddle they'd solved at the beginning. This small room was a cave of wonders, and these chests contained history's light.

"Let's go," he said.

Abi opened the other door, which led them outside the House of Wisdom, down by the river. A small boat waited there, and they loaded the chests of books into it. Then Abi and Tusi climbed aboard, and Abi used the oars to slide them out into the river's current.

"Wait!" Tusi said. "What about the children?"

"They have a very special boat of their own," Abi said,

smiling. "One that sails backward up the river."

Riq, Sera, and Dak waved at the two scholars. Abi's grin never fell as he waved back, but Tusi simply looked completely confused. Once the scholars were safely away from the House of Wisdom, Sera pulled the SQuare back out.

"New coordinates," she said. "Give me the Ring."

Riq handed it over to her. As she punched in the data, he looked up at the smoke rising into the air from within the House of Wisdom, the ashes carried over their heads into the river. The destruction of Baghdad had begun. But it would not be a complete destruction, not anymore. Many of its books, its wisdom and knowledge, would survive.

"Ready!" Sera said.

The three of them took hold of the Infinity Ring. As the device hummed in his hand, and the world began to shimmer and break apart in a shower of sparks, Riq thought back to what Abi had said.

Riq was making choices *now*.

That had to count for something.

Epilogue

SERA BLINKED.

The smoke and the burning House of Wisdom were gone, but they were still standing on the banks of a wide river. This was clearly not the Tigris, though. This river was lined with green trees. It was summer here, and the warm, humid air stuck to Sera's skin. Insects buzzed around them, and frogs croaked from the mud.

"Where are we?" Dak asked. "What river is this?"

Sera checked the SQuare. "The Mississippi. It's the summer of 1804."

"1804?" Dak got that familiar look in his eye.

Sera smiled. "Yes, 1804." She glanced at Riq, who seemed ready to shut Dak down. But since she and Dak had talked back in Hulagu's palace, she found she wasn't so bothered by Dak's enthusiasm. "Please, tell us about 1804."

"Well"—Dak cleared his throat—"that was the year the Louisiana Expedition left from St. Louis."

Right. Sera remembered something about that from school. "Go on."

Dak beamed. "President Jefferson had just acquired the Louisiana Purchase, which was this huge territory of land. He basically doubled the size of the United States. But he didn't really know what was out there, so he sent an expedition to explore. They were supposed to travel along the Missouri River and find a route to the Pacific Ocean."

"Supposed to?" Riq echoed.

"Yeah," Dak said. "But it was a complete disaster. Nobody made it back alive."

The three of them looked at one another. It was another life-or-death situation—this time in the wilderness, far from the comforts of anything like the House of Wisdom.

Dak continued. "What happened to the expedition is a mystery. Jefferson believed all kinds of crazy rumors about the West. He thought there were mammoths out there, and volcanoes, and mountains made of salt."

"Mammoths have been extinct for more than four thousand years at this point," Sera said.

"Yup," Dak said. "We know that now, but when the explorers failed to return, nobody knew what to believe. All they could say for sure was that the territory was dangerous. It was declared off-limits for decades. Jefferson was disgraced because he'd spent all this money. The country was mad at him, and he only served one term as president—" Dak paused.

"What is it?" Sera asked.

"It's just . . ." Dak's eyebrows creased together. He looked worried. "I have to remember to question everything now. Everything I thought I knew about history."

"Like what?" Riq asked.

"Like the Louisiana Expedition. What if it wasn't simply a failure? What if it was *sabotaged*? What if the SQ got involved, and they ruined Jefferson's reputation on purpose? Doesn't that seem like something they would do?"

Sera looked out over the smooth river flowing past. "That seems *exactly* like something they would do."

"There should be a fort somewhere around here," Dak said. "Camp Wood. It's where the expedition really got started, on the outskirts of St. Louis."

"I entered the coordinates carefully," Sera said. "It has to be close."

"Then that's where we should begin," Riq said. "Let's look around. Just, uh, be on the lookout for bears."

They started up the bank of the river, moving slowly through the trees and the underbrush. Birds skimmed the water and sang from the branches overhead. Sera had to admit, after the desert it was nice to be in a place that was so full of life. Even if some of it wanted to eat her.

They hadn't gone very far when Riq held up his hand to stop them. He pointed ahead, and through the trees Sera glimpsed the log wall of a fort in the distance. It looked just like the paintings she had seen of the

American frontier. Tall tree trunks stood tightly together, sharpened at the top like a row of gigantic pencils.

"I think that's Camp Wood," Dak whispered. He motioned toward a cluster of cabins and cottages that stood between them and the fort. "And this must be St. Louis. It's a total frontier town in this era. It's the edge of civilization, as far as the Americans of the time are concerned."

Something about the place felt sinister to Sera. "Do you think there are any Time Wardens this far west?"

"It's definitely possible," Dak said. "If the SQ sabotaged the expedition, they probably have an agent here. Unless he's on the road with Lewis and Clark."

Riq turned to Dak. "Lewis and Clark?"

"Right," Dak said. "Meriwether Lewis and William Clark. Jefferson put them in charge of the expedition. They were last seen leaving Camp Wood."

Riq smirked. "What do you want to bet the Break has something to do with helping these Lewis and Clark guys?"

Sera had the same thought. It was getting to the point where she could tell when something was wrong. She could almost feel it in her gut, as if she was becoming a real Hystorian with real Hystorian instincts.

"I bet you're right," Dak said. "But the expedition left weeks ago."

"Then we have some catching up to do," Riq said.

A journey into the wild American frontier sounded

exciting to Sera, but no matter what anyone said, she was *not* going to wear a dress.

And then she saw something that chilled her blood. It was carved into the wooden homes before them. It was stitched into flags and sacks of dry goods.

The symbol of the SQ was *everywhere*.

The SQ didn't just have an agent in St. Louis. They controlled the entire town.